CATS OF DESTINY

CATS OF DESTINY

BY

FAIRFAX DOWNEY

AND

PAUL BROWN

WITH PEN-AND-INK ILLUSTRATIONS BY

PAUL BROWN

Living Book Press

CONTENTS

A LEGEND OF THE CAT

Once a man who loved cats was saddened that there was no mention of them whatever in the Bible. Reverently he took his pen and wrote this story in the spirit and language of the Scriptures.

As Jesus entered a certain village he saw a young cat which had none to care for her, and she was hungry and cried unto him, and he took her up, and put her inside his garment, and she lay in his bosom.

And when he came into the village he set food and drink before the cat, and she ate and drank, and showed thanks unto him.

And he gave her unto one of his disciples who was a widow, whose name was Lorenza, and she took care of her. And some of the people said, This man careth for all creatures. Are they his brothers and sisters that he should love them? And he said unto them, verily these are your fellow creatures of the great household of God; yea, they are your brothers and sisters, having the same breath of life in the Eternal. And whosoever careth for one of the least of these, and giveth it to eat and drink in its need, the same doeth it unto me; and whoso willingly suffereth one of these to be in want, and defendeth it not when evilly treated, suffereth the evil as done unto me.

The Rev. G. T. Ouseley:
Gospel of the Holy Twelve

MAU

SACRED IN EGYPT

JEWELS gleaming in her pointed ears, an ornate, golden necklace glistening upon the striped, short-haired fur of her sleek coat, Mau stared down from the temple wall. Below in the streets of the ancient Egyptian city of Bubastis, built upon an island in the lower Nile, a dreadful, stricken silence had fallen.

Mau's topaz eyes saw that one of her own kind, a cat of the city, had been killed. Some foreigner—a prince or wealthy nobleman from his splendid raiment—had driven his chariot over the animal. Suddenly the silence was shattered by an angry roar from a thousand throats. Soldiers, priests, shop-keepers, even slaves rushed in to surround the chariot and the limp body behind it. Mau watched the foreign man's gestures, first calm, then alarmed, explaining the killing as an accident. She caught sight, too, of the shining coins he offered in recompense. Not all the gold in his realm nor his rank could save him from the consequences of his impious deed. He had slain a cat, and it did not matter that his victim was a family pet and no temple cat like Mau. All cats were sacred in mighty Egypt.

Inscrutable, tail twitching slightly, Mau saw the mob close

Paul Brown

in with clubs and stones and clutching hands. Once only the foreigner shrieked, then he was battered and crushed and torn limb from limb. Owners of the dead cat carried it tenderly home, shaving their eyebrows in token of mourning and giving the body to be mummified and buried in the cemetery of cats.

As swift punishment had been visited on the slayer, so also any foreigner caught attempting to take a cat out of the country would fare ill. When cats were successfully smuggled abroad, Egyptians made every effort to recover them, sending regular missions to ransom them from slavery, save them from profane treatment and bring them home. So closely guarded were the sacred cats of Egypt that not until the time of the Roman Empire did they spread to other lands and become common domestic animals.

Mau descended from the wall to stroll through the temple. Priests and attendants made way for her as would the Pharoah himself, for the name she bore, along with the other holy cats of the shrine, signified a seer—one who could pierce the veil of the future. Graven images hewn in her likeness sat at the feet of statues of Bast, the cat-headed goddess of this temple—Bast, the moon deity who held the sun in her eyes at night as cats do. Cat-headed too was Sekhmet, fierce goddess of war, and though the face of the Sphinx was human, its body was that of the great cat, the lion.

Mau in her lithe beauty trod with a lordly tread as if she realized her divinity, ranking with that of other sacred animals of Egypt: the bull, the ram, the ibis, the crocodile, and the hawk. So through centuries following cats would bear themselves on occasion—mysterious, untouchable, aloof. Mau's life was all veneration and dignified luxury, with priests ministering to her every want, feeding her choice fish and bread soaked in milk. But in the stillness of the night she put aside the mantle of her sanctity and, motionless and stealthy, she crouched in wait within the temple granary beside other cats of Bast. When hungry rats and mice ventured from their holes, the cats pounced and slew. Thus they fulfilled the function which had made the cat first precious, then holy, in Egypt, granary of the ancient world. Modern scientists have estimated that one pair of rats in three years can multiply into 600,000 and that such a horde can devour as much food as 64,000 men. Had it not been for Mau and her tribe, rodents would have consumed much of the rich harvest of the Nile Delta, and famine have raged oftener in the land of the Pharaohs.

Dwelling in temples like Mau, in palaces, houses and huts, the cats of Egypt lived out their lives, worshipped and beloved. If fire broke out in a home, they were rescued first. Kept from harm, most of them died natural deaths and were interred with ceremony in vast cat burial grounds such as Beni-Hassan, where one day the mummies of 180,000 would be excavated.

For Mau when her time came, and for other temple or royal cats like her, only a funeral of magnificence was suitable. Skillful embalmers preserved her body with all the care given persons of high prestige. They wound strips of fine linen about her, layer upon layer. Her mummy was coated and gilded, and eyes of alabaster were inset before it was sealed in a bronze case, cast in her shape. And placed about it in the tomb for the sustenance of her ka, her spirit, in the hereafter were mummies of mice.

MUEZZA

PET OF THE PROPHET

A WHITE cat slept deeply on the broad, outspread sleeve of the robe of her master, seated on the flat rooftop of a dwelling in the city of Damascus. Because she belonged to the dark man with the burning eyes on whose garment she lay curled, Muezza was held in high honor. She was the beloved pet of the Prophet Mohammed, founder of a fiercely zealous religion which had spread beyond the borders of Arabia and on deeper into Asia, a faith destined to flood through Africa and on into Christendom.

Followers of Mohammed often had watched him gently lift Muezza so that she could finish her bowl of milk, or hold her in his arms while he preached to his disciples. It was no wonder that Muezza, sharing the veneration accorded her master, was surnamed Abuhareira—ancestress of cats—and that she had won kindness and mercy for her kind. Here in Damascus there was an endowed hospital for cats.

As Mohammed meditated, and Muezza slumbered by his side, the sun sank slowly. It was the hour of evening prayer. Muezzins appeared on the balconies of towering minarets and called the faithful to worship. "There is no God but Allah," their echoing voices chanted. "Great is Allah, and Mohammed is his prophet."

Mohammed stirred and half rose to obey the summons of the priests. Least of all could he neglect them but must spread his prayer rug and prostrate himself toward Mecca, decreed a holy shrine because it was his birthplace. Yet, looking down at the white cat in peaceful repose on his sleeve, he could not bring himself to disturb her.

Quietly he drew his knife. A slash of its keen blade, and the sleeve was severed. Only then did the Prophet answer the call to prayer, leaving Muezza still soundly asleep upon the cloth.

The tale of Mohammed's fond consideration of his cat was told in many a market and caravanserai. Story-tellers, embroidering it, related that when Muezza woke from her nap on the sleeve, she walked to her master, rubbed against his legs and purred her thanks for his thoughtfulness. Whereupon the Prophet, understanding that she was showing her appreciation of his deed, passed a hand three times over her arched back, thus giving her kind immunity forever from any harm on that part of the body. So that is why cats, falling or dropped from a height, are said to land on their feet.

Muezza's prestige as the pet of the Prophet lived on after her, and for her sake Mohammedans everywhere cherished cats. Anyone who mistreated one was scorned or beaten, for Mohammed had set the example when he commanded the punishment of a pitiless woman who tied up her cat to starve, refusing to free it so that "it might eat the reptiles of the ground"—lizards and snakes. Since Muezza had lain in the bosom of the Prophet, cats were allowed to enter mosques, where they were welcomed and fondled. In the great city of Constantinople,

captured from the Christians, Moslems gave their cats the same fond care they did their children. The powerful Mameluke Sultan of Egypt, El Daher Beybars, founded an asylum for the homeless cats of Cairo. Two or three pussies, in charge of an old woman called Mother of Cats, always traveled camelback with the caravan which each year bore the Sacred Carpet back and forth between Cairo and Mecca, and that custom is said to have been founded as a memorial to Muezza.

An Arab chronicler borrowed the story of Noah from the Bible and added a tale of the creation of the cat, relating that when mice overran the Ark, Allah caused the lion to sneeze, and the cat ran out of his nostrils. "From that time," proclaimed the scribe, "the mouse has been timid and has hidden in holes."

Christian artists adopted that Arab legend. Ignoring the fact that cats are not once mentioned in the Bible—perhaps because they were sacred in Egypt, hated land of Hebrew bondage—a Renaissance painter depicted a large and dignified pussy at the head of the procession of animals leaving the Ark after the flood. Another painting portrayed a cat lying in the place of honor at the feet of Adam and Eve, and still another showed one remaining in the Garden of Eden while the first man and woman were being driven forth.

Although the tradition founded by Muezza inspired Christian artists, it failed to win kindness to cats of Christian countries. During cruel centuries, thousands of the poor creatures were branded familiars of demons and witches and tortured and killed. But in Moslem lands the memory of Mohammed's white cat blessed the feline race. And to this day nurses in Cairo tell children the story of her undisturbed rest on the severed sleeve of the Prophet.

DICK WHITTINGTON'S CAT

LORD MAYOR'S FORTUNE

DICK WHITTINGTON kept the cat he had bought in his garret room in the London house of the rich merchant for whom he worked as scullion. The orphan boy was certain that he could not have spent the penny he had earned by blacking boots in a better way than the purchase of this affectionate companion. The cat changed his cramped quarters from a place of lonely despair. She curled up warmly on his lap and purred and, while he was asleep, rid the room of swarms of rats and mice. By day Dick hid his cat in a cupboard so that the cook and other servants, who cuffed and kicked him as he went about his duties in the kitchen of the Fitzwarren household, would not abuse her.

Despite the cat's company, Dick's lot was hard, and there seemed but little prospect of his making the fortune he had come trudging from his home in Shropshire to seek. Yet his employer, Sir Ivo Fitzwarren, his wife, and their lovely daughter, Alice, were kind to the lad of fourteen. And there finally came a day when the merchant, fitting out his ship, *Unicorn*, for a venture to Algiers, offered all his servants, including Dick, a chance to share in the profits by investing their savings in English goods which would be put aboard for trade with the Algerians.

Alas, poor Dick possessed nothing to send. He already had spent the penny, all he had been able to save.

Hold, he did own something—his beloved cat! Tears running down his cheeks, the boy brought his pet and entrusted her to the shipmaster.

Lonelier than ever, Dick returned to his tasks. Months passed, and the cook's brutality at last grew so intolerable he could endure it no longer. Dreams and hopes faded, he ran away and retraced his steps toward his old home. Reaching Highgate Hill, he sat down wearily on a boulder which to this day is called "Whittington's Stone." It was All Hallows Day, and the Bow bells began pealing merrily, their strokes seeming to sound a message for the listening lad.

"Turn again, Whittington,
Thrice Lord Mayor of London."

Dick jumped up from the stone and strode back to the Fitzwarren house.

Meanwhile his cat had fulfilled her destiny. On the voyage she made herself such a favorite of the shipmaster that he would allow no one else to care for her. At Algiers he took her ashore when he was invited to a state banquet by the Dey. As sumptuous dishes were set before the guests seated on divans, rats infesting the palace dashed in and out and snatched the food from the very platters. Thereupon the captain held up the eagerly squirming cat and was granted permission to let her loose. That experienced mouser pounced on the vermin and slew them right and left, to the great delight of the Dey.

At once he bargained for the cat, and an old tale relates that as her price he "sent on board the ship the choicest commodities, consisting of gold, jewels, and silks." Nor is the story as exaggerated as it seems, for in certain countries at that time where rats and mice were a pest and there were no native cats, imported ones were worth their weight in gold.

So Dick, summoned by the bells, hastened back to the merchant's dwelling and learned the *Unicorn* had returned, and his venture had repaid him many hundredfold, while his cat had become a cherished member of the Dey's court.

From that day the lad's fortunes rose higher and higher. He became a merchant like Sir Ivo, dealing in velvets, damask, and cloth of gold. He and the fair Alice were married, and just as the bells had foretold, Dick Whittington was thrice elected Lord Mayor of London. Out of his wealth he made large loans to two Kings of England, Henry IV and Henry V.

For three hundred years after Whittington's death in 1423, the story of his cat went unquestioned. Later savants labeled it a legend, in spite of the facts that it had lived long as a tradition and that a stone statue of a boy with a cat in his arms was found in Whittington's house when it was remodeled. But many others always will believe that the story of Dick Whittington and his cat is as true as it is charming.

CAT OF SIR HENRY WYATT

PRISONER'S FRIEND

A CAT played a part in the War of the Roses, that bloody struggle fought for the throne of England. Her name has not survived but the memory of her deeds was preserved by the grateful knight whose life she saved.

Sir Henry Wyatt chose the red rose, the badge of Lancaster, against the white of York and suffered grievously from his choice, for York prevailed, and the crown finally fell to Richard III. That ruthless monarch sought to seduce the able Sir Henry to his service and, failing, the King flung the loyal Lancastrian into the grim Tower of London.

Wyatt was tortured on the rack, and mustard was forced down his throat, yet he would not yield. He might well then have been slain, for in that very prison Richard had ordered the slaughter of two boy princes who stood in his path. Instead of a quick death, Sir Henry was left to freeze in a cold, narrow, bedless cell with prison fare so scant he was slowly starving.

One day a cat crept through the grating into his dungeon. A lonely stray, she craved human companionship, and the prisoner found as much comfort in her company as she in his.

"He was glad of her, laid her in his bosom to warm him, and by making much of her, won her love," so says an old chronicle of the time.

Thereafter the cat came to visit him several times a day. Sensing his hunger, she brought him a pigeon she had caught in a neighboring dovecote. The thin and wasted knight hid the bird and summoned the keeper to complain again of his meager rations, begging that in God's mercy he be granted a little meat to keep him alive.

"I durst not do better," the jailer protested.

"But if I can provide any, will you promise to dress it for me?" Sir Henry asked.

"I may well enough. You are safe in that matter," the keeper answered. He kept his word, and when given the pigeon, he plucked and cooked it for his charge.

Again and again the cat brought fat pigeons to her friend, saving him from the starvation which would have been his lot.

The prisoner was released when King Richard, crushed by revolt, was killed in battle, and though Wyatt, in the succeeding reigns of King Henry VII and Henry VIII, rose too high posts, he never forgot the faithful cat nor her kind. People noticed that he would make as much of cats as other men of their spaniels and hounds.

A portrait shows him in his Tower cell, his cat pulling a pigeon through the barred window, and at the bottom of the painting is inscribed this tribute:

> "This Knight with hunger, cold, and care neere starv'd,
>   pincht, pyned away,
> A sillie [weak] Beast did feede, heate, cheere, with dyett,
>   warmth, and play."

SATHAN

FAMILIAR OF WITCHES

WHEN the Devil came seeking mortals as his prey, he appeared as a black dog, a toad, or a serpent, so people avowed. But his favorite form when he wished to serve as a companion to witches was that of a cat. And never, declared superstitious, sixteenth-century England, had the fiend wreaked more havoc than in the years he prowled about in a feline shape that bore his own name, Sathan.

Sathan was a white, spotted cat whose baleful glare frightened the folk of the Chelmsford countryside. Some of them shuddered with that strange, real dread of cats which has been recognized since the time of the Greeks, whose language had a word for them: ailurophobes—persons who hate the creature that waves its tail.

Once the evidence of Sathan's wicked work was seen, no one ever doubted that he was a witch-cat. It was whispered that he had come from abroad and swum the Channel to reach England. Others insisted that he had craftily used a bishop, about to take ship from France, as his passport and had arrived perched on the prelate's shoulder. Actually the cat was given Elizabeth Francis by her grandmother, who at the same time was reputed to have taught her granddaughter to renounce God and practice witchcraft.

Sathan, curled in a basket, spoke to his mistress in an uncanny, hollow voice. While he partook of milk and bread, it was only when Elizabeth let him lap a drop of her own blood that he would perform an evil service. First she employed the cat to bewitch a neighbor's hog which sickened and died. Then she demanded riches of Sathan, and lo, a flock of eighteen black and white sheep was found grazing in her pasture, though later all mysteriously vanished. Something of more permanence, a wealthy husband, was next demanded of the cat. There Sathan's spells failed. He could not force Andrew Byles to marry his mistress, but the man for his stubbornness soon lost all his goods and died.

Soon a husband, though less well-off than Byles, was provided, but the couple quarreled, and a daughter born to them cried constantly. The witch caused Sathan to kill the infant and to lame her spouse by changing into a toad and hiding in his shoe. Dreadful events multiplied. Valuable cattle perished, and at length black arts were the death of Elizabeth's husband, and then of a neighbor and his wife.

Witch-hunters now commenced the merciless persecutions which in England and later in America would send hundreds of unfortunate women to the gallows or the stake—victims of coincidence and of their own and neighbors' spite, whipped up by cruel and senseless superstition. Finally Elizabeth was tried at Chelmsford in 1556, confessed to witchcraft and was hanged.

But Sathan, which had served his mistress with malignant fidelity for more than fifteen years, escaped. Just before her arrest she had traded him for a cake, along with her knowledge of sorcery, to Mother Agnes Waterhouse. Again the neighbor-

hood was afflicted with one misfortune after another, as Sathan in return for his reward of a drop of the new witch's blood obeyed her commands. A brewer who had refused Mother Waterhouse a bribe found his beer spoiled. Butter soured in churns. A hog, three geese, and a widow's cow died after their owners had fallen out with the old woman whose familiar was a spotted cat. Nobody managed to catch Sathan, though elsewhere men wounded cats found lurking at the scene of a disaster, and next day the women to whom the cats belonged were seen bearing cuts or bruises.

Hysterical panic spread through rural England. It was said that Sathan warned Mother Waterhouse to stay home or she would be hanged or burned, but she did not heed him and was dragged before the witchcraft court. At the trial, Queen Bess's attorney demanded of her:

"When did thy cat suck thy blood?"

"Never!" she made denial. But plain on her nose and face were marks where she was accused of pricking herself to feed the demon. In the year 1566 hangmen dropped a noose around her neck and swung her high against the sky.

Sathan vanished. There is no record that he shared the cruel fate of countless other cats which through the Middle Ages and later supposedly more civilized times were dipped in oil and set afire, hurled from towers, beaten to death with whips and knotted ropes, scalded and flayed alive because the poor creatures were suspected of being instruments of the Devil.

On Hallowe'en it is said to be a black cat that rides the broomstick behind a beak-nosed, hook-chinned old woman in a conical hat. But it might better be a white, spotted one in the image of Sathan, the most famous witch-cat of them all.

MANX

THEREBY HANGS NO TAIL

"Are you aware that the cats have got
    No tails in the Isle of Man?
In England, Ireland, Scotland, Wales,
All the cats have lovely tails.
It is a gross injustice—
    To right it is our plan.
Oh, are you aware that the cats have got
    No tails in the Isle of Man?"

So runs a jolly song about Manx cats which, true enough, have no tails. And ever since the first tailless cats appeared on the Isle of Man, people have been trying to explain their taillessness.

One story tells that it came about when the Ark was almost ready to float on the rising waters of the Flood, and Noah was peering out in search of a missing animal—one of the cats. At last through the drenching downpour of rain he came scampering aboard. Noah called him inside but slammed the door shut so hastily that his tail was caught and cut off; what follows is best told in an old rhyme.

> "Said the cat, and he was Manx,
>> 'Oh, Captain Noah, wait!
> I'll catch the mice to give you thanks,
>> And pay for being late.'
> So the cat got in but oh,
> His tail was a bit too slow."

Or if you like to believe that Noah must have been kind to animals even when he was in a hurry, you'll prefer another version:

> "Noah, sailing o'er the seas,
>> Ran fast aground on Ararat.
> His dog then made a spring and took
>> The tail from off a pussy cat.
> Puss through the window quick did fly,
>> And bravely through the waters swam,
> Nor ever stopped till high and dry
>> She landed on the Isle of Man."

A wise cat of the Isle of Man is given the credit in a second yarn. She and all the other Manxes in those early days boasted beautiful, bushy tails which, alas, were proving fatal. Warriors killed every cat they could lay hands on and fastened its tail on their helmets as a crest. Recognizing this alarming trend, one surviving cat, about to become a mother, fled to a refuge in the hills. When her five kittens were born, she bit off their tails. As soon as they grew to cathood, she explained her deed and advised her offspring to play safe and go do likewise when they had kittens.

Once upon a time there was a beautiful Oriental princess, begins a third tale. About to bathe in a lake on the palace grounds, she feared she might lose her rings, so she slipped them on to the tail of her cat. But her pet, wandering along the shore, lowered its tail, and the rings slid into the water.

Next time the princess went swimming she did the same thing with her new rings but tied a loop in her cat's tail above the jewelry, making it as secure as if it were the royal treasury. So the princess and her cat, although its kittens had kinks in their tails or no tails at all, lived happily ever after.

It is a fact that a breed of kink-tailed cats and cats without tails—tails lost perhaps because of the weakness of the kinks did develop in the Orient. Some of those tailless ones were carried westward in the Islamic Conquest and remained in Spain after the Saracens were driven out. And that leads to the most believable story of all as to how such cats reached the Isle of Man.

Cats without tails are said to have been aboard the ships of the mighty Armada, sent by Philip II of Spain to conquer England. When sudden tempests and Queen Elizabeth's gallant little fleet smote the Spaniards, down sank the great galleons to the bottom of the Channel or were dashed ashore along the coast. Several wrecks from the Armada that had been called invincible broke up on a reef, thenceforth known as Spanish Rock, close to the Isle of Man. All hands were lost, but the ships' cats leaped clear, reached the Rock and at low tide made their way ashore. Natives of Man took in the castaways—big, handsome tabbies and blacks, with long hind legs and not a trace of a tail.

Tailless, Manx cats flourish to this day.

FISHING CAT

HE NAMED A STREET

THE big cat scampered for safety, as the Seine roared through Paris. Swollen by spring freshets of the year 1658, the river had changed from a peaceful stream meandering through the city into a raging torrent. It flooded islands in its course and burst its banks to sweep flimsy, medieval dwellings from their foundations.

After the flood subsided, the cat, houseless and hungry like many Parisians, wandered back to the Left Bank where his home had stood. No one fed him, and the rats and mice had been drowned.

Idly at first, then intently, he watched men gather around the open cellars with poles and lines. Seine fishermen were a familiar sight, but these anglers ignored the river to cast into the water-filled cellars. Hardly had they dropped hooks when sinkers bobbed under, and poles were jerked up to land silvery fish, flashing in the sun. The flood had turned each excavation into a splendid fishing preserve.

The cat sniffed hungrily and mewed. Fish were fine eating. When nobody offered him a share, he stole up the edge of a

PaulBrown

cellar. Fishermen glanced up with interest at this cat which, unlike most of his kind, seemed unafraid of water. A swift, clawed paw flashed downward to scoop up a fish, then another, and the meal problem was neatly solved.

Day after day the cat joined the human anglers. Word spread, and people thronged to watch the clever feline fisherman. Perhaps he dove in at times to make his catch, since some cats are good swimmers.

So great an impression did he make, a street of the vicinity was named for him. It had first been *Ruelle des Etuves*—Alley of the Ovens—then *Rue du Renard*—Street of the Fox, but now it became *Rue du Chat Qui Pêche*—Street of the Fishing Cat. A sign, depicting the cat in action, long swung from one of the rebuilt houses.

Through three centuries the street has borne its name. Jutting out to the Seine and connecting *Quai Saint-Michel* with *Rue de la Huchette*, it is one of the narrowest and shortest of streets— thirty paces long by two wide—but the tiny thoroughfare is famous, and many a visitor to the Left Bank is attracted by its quaint name, commemorating the prowess of the fishing cat.

More celebrity still came to the cat and his street when it was made the title of a novel by Jolán Földes, published in 1937. The story's heroine, like many a tourist in Paris today, was fascinated by the *Rue du Chat Qui Pêche*. "When Anna was young, she often wove fancies about its name," Földes wrote. "An old, fat tomcat, with a big moustache like those of the other anglers who sit two paces from each other on the square stones of the Seine banks, their legs hanging down and reflected in the river. There the old tomcat sits, with his big moustache and a pair of spectacles on his nose, a cap on his head, holding the rod gravely and dropping the line into the water."

JEOFFRY

A CAT IN BEDLAM

IN Bedlam, London's prison for the insane, a haunt of terror and hopelessness, the cat Jeoffry crouched by his master's side. Men and women, ragged and verminous, peered through the barred windows or lay in dank straw on the floors, for the eighteenth century knew no other way to treat poor, demented folk than to shut them up in prison. The violent ones clanked fetters which chained them to the wall, and their moans and shrieks rose to a pitch which would make the name of Bedlam a common word for uproar and turmoil. Yet the cat Jeoffry, despite the torture to his fine-strung nerves by the constant tumult, would not abandon his master, Christopher Smart.

"Poor Smart," they called him now. Once he had been a scholar and don at Cambridge, a writer of promise, and the friend of Johnson, Goldsmith, Garrick, and Gray. Then he had taken the path of the drunkard and spendthrift, resorting to literary hack work to eke out a miserable existence for his wife, two daughters, and himself, and sinking deeper into the depths. A religious mania seized him, and he took to kneel-

ing in the streets and babbling prayers until they clapped him into Bedlam.

Within that place of dark despair, Jeoffry gave his master such companionship and solace as a cat had given Sir Henry Wyatt in the Tower and as one had bestowed on the Italian poet, Torquato Tasso, when the Duke of Ferrara imprisoned him as a madman in the dungeon of Santa Anna. As Tasso in a sonnet to his cat begged it to lend him the light of its eyes through the dark night to write his verses by, so Christopher Smart may have pleaded with Jeoffry. For while the self-wrecked man watched his cat's gravity and waggery and his elegant quickness in pursuit of mice—while he felt the warm comfort of his pet on his lap—slowly the mists of madness began to clear, and the urge to write returned.

On scraps of paper Smart composed his one great work: the long, mystical poem entitled "A Song to David," in which a stanza devoted to Jeoffry contains some of the most remarkable lines ever written to a cat.

> "For I will consider my cat Jeoffry.
> For he is the servant of the living God, duly and daily
> serving him.

Smart's poem praised Jeoffry's cleanliness and marveled that though he was quickest to his mark of any creature, there was nothing sweeter than his peace when at rest. He gratefully told how Jeoffry had diverted him during his long confinement by learning to fetch and carry, jump over a stick, and catch a cork and toss it again.

> "For he is of the tribe of the Tiger.
> For the Cherub Cat is a term of the Angel Tiger.

For he has the subtlety and hissing of a serpent, which in
    goodness he suppresses.
For he will not do destruction, if he is well-fed, neither
    will he spit without provocation.
For he purrs in thankfulness, when God tells him he's a
    good cat.
For every house is incomplete without him and a bless-
    ing is
For he is an instrument for the children to learn benevo-
    lence upon, lacking in the spirit..."

Poor Smart won release from Bedlam, but his spirit would
rise no more to the heights, and he died in debtor's prison. Yet
he had earned lasting fame with his one original and powerful
poem, inspired in part by a cat.

SELIMA

FATE AND FISH

Selima, "demurest of the tabby kind," leaned over the rim of the big goldfish bowl. A slip, a splash, and in she plunged to perish in a watery grave, yet to live for all time in one of the most popular poems in English literature.

She was a beauty, was Selima, and Horace Walpole had prized her most among the fine cats that graced his villa on Strawberry Hill, outside Twickenham, England.

When Selima met her fate, her owner wrote the sad news to his friend and Eton schoolmate, Thomas Gray. While the cat's name might have survived through mention in those brilliant letters for which Walpole was noted, greater fame was in store for her. Gray replied that he was immortalizing Selima in a poem rather too long for an epitaph. It was a light and sparkling lament for the deceased Selima: *Ode on the Death of a Favorite Cat, Drowned in a Tub of Goldfishes,* and Gray might have been present at the tragedy so vividly did he describe it.

His pen pictured Selima crouched above the bowl and gazing down as into a little lake. "Her conscious tail her joy declared"—nothing except the human tongue is more eloquent

than a cat's tail. Below she beheld "two angel forms—the Genii of the stream"—a pair of gliding goldfish. The fierce elation of a huntress, the lure of the forbidden, seized upon her. "A whisker first and then a claw she stretched in vain to reach the prize." Was she not both feminine and feline?

> "What female heart can gold despise?
>   What cat's averse to fish?"

Then retribution and poetic justice!

> "The slippery verge her feet beguiled,
>   She tumbled headlong in.

> "Eight times emerging from the flood
> She mewed to every watery god,
>   Some speedy aid to send."

None answered. "A Favorite has no friend." Craving her gleaming prey, she had learned too late that all that glisters is not gold.

The ode to the departed Selima was launched on a triumphant course to be reprinted and quoted countless times. It has been given such illustration as the amusing engravings which show Destiny cutting the nine threads of Selima's lives while mice make merry, and a scene where her wraith is ferried across the Styx, back arched, tail fluffed and spitting at the guardian of the nether regions, the three-headed dog, Cerberus.

Appropriately the poem was inscribed on a bowl which "China's gayest art had dyed," the very bowl wherein Selima had drowned. After Gray's death, Walpole placed it on a pedestal in the hall of his villa to commemorate his friend and his cat.

HODGE

DR. JOHNSON'S PET

THE black cat Hodge scrambled up his master's well-filled waistcoat to have his back stroked and his tail gently pulled, and Dr. Johnson obliged, half smiling, half whistling. The good Doctor, compiler of a monumental dictionary, author, and arbiter of English letters, might roar at people who annoyed him, but he was fond of cats.

James Boswell, seated across the chamber, observed that Hodge received the attentions "apparently with great satisfaction." Everything Dr. Johnson did or said was carefully noted by this admirer who would perpetuate his fame in one of the world's great biographies, and Hodge would share celebrity in *The Life of Samuel Johnson, LL.D.*

"A fine cat," remarked Boswell and might well have added, "if you like cats." Hodge made him nervously uncomfortable, since Boswell was an ailurophobe. Not a few people share this strange dread which causes some to faint or rush from a room where a cat, even unseen, is present. But since Hodge belonged to Dr. Johnson, he must be a fine cat.

"Well yes, Sir," the lexicographer agreed, "but I have had

Fish

cats whom I like better than this." Then he looked down at his pet to perceive that his words seemed to have put Hodge out of countenance and hastened to amend, "but he is a very fine cat, a very fine cat indeed."

Dr. Johnson returned the black cat's affection. When Hodge fell ill and could eat only oysters, the ponderous Doctor trudged a distance to the market to buy them for him. Always considerate of servants, he would not send his valet Francis who might show resentment at being ordered to run an errand for an animal.

Once Boswell warned his revered friend of the despicable state of a young gentleman of good family who was running about town shooting cats. Instantly the Doctor sprang to the defense of his pet and rumbled: "But Hodge shan't be shot; no, no, Hodge shall not be shot."

Hodge lived out his life with his famous owner, and when the cat came to the end of his days, Johnson, on the advice of his friend, Mrs. Thrale, bought valerian, a catnip-like herb, to soothe his pet's last hours.

It is not only in Boswell's pages that Hodge survives. Recently this elegy in his honor by Percival Stockdale was rediscovered.

> "Let not the honest muse disdain
> For Hodge to wake the plaintive strain.
> Shall poets prostitute their lays
> In offering venal Statesmen praise;
> By them shall flowers Parnassian bloom
> Around the tyrant's gaudy tomb;
> And shall not Hodge's memory claim
> Of innocence the candid fame;
> Shall not his worth a poem fill,
> Who never thought, nor uttered ill;
> Who, by his master when caressed

Warmly his gratitude expressed;
And never failed his thanks to purr
Whene'er he stroked his sable fur?
    The general conduct if we trace
Of our articulating race,
Hodge's example we shall find
A keen reproof to human kind...
He never filched a single groat,
Nor bilked a taylor of a coat;
His garb when first he drew his breath
His dress through life, his shroud in death...
    But wouldst thou, son of Adam, learn
Praise from thy noblest powers to earn;
Dost thou, with generous pride, aspire
Thy nature's glory to acquire?
Then in thy life exert the man,
With moral deeds adorn the span;
Let virtue in thy bosom lodge;
Or wish thou hadst been born a Hodge."

MINETTE

MODEL FOR THE CAT RAPHAEL

MINETTE, most dearly cherished cat of Gottfried Mind, the artist, was in desperate danger. At all costs her master must protect her. His other cats, even the helpless little kittens, he might have to yield up, but Minette—no!—they should never take her from him.

Throughout the city of Berne in Switzerland a terrible massacre was in progress, with police and citizens shooting and clubbing to death every cat they could find. The merciless slaughter was invading every home, and not a single pussy would be spared. True, it was not senseless cruelty. A frightful epidemic of hydrophobia was raging among cats of the city in this year of 1809. Jaws slavering, crazed, rabid, the creatures dashed about, attacking every living thing they met—their own kind, other animals, people. To all their bite was death. There was no cure then known, and their victims, infected by their madness, spread it further before they perished in convulsions.

Killers of cats would be coming soon to search Mind's dwelling for Minette and the rest. They knew there were always cats about the artist, for they had been his chosen subject since the

day when as a young apprentice he had been caught staring at the sketch of one made by his master. "Can you draw a better one?" the elder artist demanded, annoyed by his pupil's critical gaze. The lad's swift strokes convinced the teacher, who ordered him to elaborate his drawing and then included it in the painting. From that moment Mind had risen to fame as a portrayer of cats.

Minette long had been his favorite model. It was she chiefly that had won him his reputation and the name of the "Cat Raphael." His portraits limned her appealing expression, the glossiness of her white coat marked with brown and black, her graceful attitudes, the suppleness of her body undulating beneath its fur. She was constantly by his side, under his studying eyes, or crouched in his lap. Her kittens climbed on to his shoulders and the back of his neck. Rather than disturb his friends, Mind would sit stooped before his easel for hours; for him contented purring was reward enough. While he worked, he carried on conversations with Minette with gestures and words and was certain she understood him.

The dreaded knock of the police sounded on the door. Mind's frantic pleadings that his cats were well and safe could not save them. Duty, hard and pitiless, was done. Was that all? Searchers ransacked the dwelling to make certain no victim escaped.

Mind had hidden Minette in the most secret place he could devise. His spirit in turmoil, he watched the hunt go on. It was possible, he knew, that he might be concealing a menace to his fellow citizens—that he risked imprisonment, even death at the hands of an angry mob—but it was for the beloved Minette, not himself, that he trembled.

A hidden dog might have scratched or barked, but the wise

Minette, as if she realized her mortal peril, did not betray herself. And they never found her.

The epidemic passed, and in time cats once more appeared in Berne, solacing people who had lost their pets, performing their age-old service of ridding homes of rats and mice. Now it was safe for the beloved Minette to be brought, sleek and healthy, out of her hiding place and for Mind to acquire other cats. Again kittens gamboled in the house. Happily the artist painted them and made marvelous little sculptures of them, carved from chestnuts. These statuettes lined his mantelpiece, but unfortunately worms destroyed them.

Minette, posing often for her fond master, had little cause for jealousy. The only other creatures he would paint beside cats were bears, which came lumbering to meet him when he visited their enclosures at the zoo. To people, including agents of royalty and art connoisseurs who flocked to buy his pictures, the artist was rude, but he was always courtesy itself to pussies. It was even said he finally came to look like a cat.

Mind painted Minette and other cats often right up to the day of his death in 1814. He had never recovered from the shock of the massacre during the epidemic, and the Cat Raphael sought to make as many of his friends as he could immortal on his canvases.

RUMPEL

CAT DUELIST

FUR flew when Rumpel met his mortal enemy, the cat Hurly. The former's domain was the house, the latter's the garden, and any invasion of territory was a declaration of war. Both cats belonged to Robert Southey, England's Poet Laureate, and lines in his famous poem, "The Battle of Blenheim," referring to the English and the French, fitted his rival toms as aptly:

> "But what they fought each other for
> I could not well make out."

Rumpel came to the Southey family when his original owners, neighbors, moved away. He was a gentlemanly creature, a mixture of tabby and white. Though not handsome, he was large and well-made, with good features and an intelligent countenance. His eyes were soft and expressive, of a hue between topaz and chrysolite, and he carried his splendid tail as proudly as if it were the seat of honor in cats—which his master maintained it was.

The new cat was nameless and must be christened. Inspiration struck while the poet at breakfast was reading a Grimm

fairy tale to his children—the story of the dwarf who threatened to steal a baby princess unless her parents could discover his name in three days. You remember that they all lived happily ever after when the King, wandering in the forest, heard the dwarf reciting a verse which contained his name: Rumpelstiltzchen.

Delighted, the children named the family's new pet after the dwarf. Even that was not enough, their smiling father insisted, for so imposing a cat. He added a string of titles: The most Noble the Archduke Rumpelstiltzchen, Marquis Macbum, Earl Tomlemagne, Baron Raticide, Waowhler, and Skaratch.

Rumpel was monarch of all he surveyed in the Southey manor, Greta Hall, termed "Cats' Eden" on the poet's letterheads. It was populated by pussies bearing the names of Italian opera singers, Indian chiefs, and legendary heroes. The Poet Laureate cherished them all and wrote many fond letters and pieces about them.

But the calm of this feline paradise vanished when Rumpel met his antagonist, Hurlyburlybuss. Instantly enmity flamed high. Backs up, teeth bared, tails fuzzy with electric hostility, the duelists prepared for the fray.

"Oh, it is dreadful to hear the notes with which they prelude their encounters," Southey wrote. "The long, slow growl slowly rises until it becomes a yowl, and then it is snapped short by a sound which seems as though they were spitting fire and venom at each other." Defiance cast, conflict was joined.

Often the battle-scarred and ear-torn combatants had to be separated. But soon they were at it again, and their owner was forced to confess that "the processes of the Society for the Abolition of War were not more utterly ineffectual and helpless" than his own efforts at peace-making.

Hurly, a hardy, outdoor cat, remained master of the green and garden. Rumpel, retiring into the house as to a citadel or sanctuary, held it stoutly and enjoyed luxurious repose by the fire. Once when Hurly fell ill, Rumpel made friendly overtures which for a time were warily received. Yet as soon as Rumpel had regained his confidence and Hurly his health, warfare raged once more.

Only the sight of Southey petting other cats reconciled the enemies. The poet described in verse the emotions he was certain they were feeling.

> "Ah! little do you know how swiftly fly
> The venomed darts of feline jealousy."

The green-eyed passion drove them to despair, he guessed, and would bring them to deliver to him, if they could, a signed ultimatum that they were

> "Resolv'd we hang from yonder apple tree—
> And were not that a sad catastrophe...
> Our mutual jealousies we both disown,
> Content to share rather than lose a throne.
> The parlor—Rumpel's undisputed reign.
> Hurly's—the rest of all your wide domain...
> Resign yourself to Home, the Muse, and us.
> Scratched,
> Rumpelstiltzchen
> Hurlyburlybuss."

Death at last brought peace to the warlike Rumpel. His master, remarking that there were no catacombs on the estate, saw to it that he was decently interred in the orchard, and catnip planted on his grave.

LANGBOURNE

A FELINE KNIGHT

LANGBOURNE in his early days was a debonair cat-about-town, a regular rake and rascal of a fellow, nor was he ever discouraged by his master, Jeremy Bentham, though Bentham was an authority on law and wrote learned tomes about it.

With Langbourne at his heels, the sprightly old gentleman strode rapidly through the London streets, long white locks streaming, walking stick swinging. Bentham liked cats with no more domestic virtues than he himself possessed—he was wifeless, childless and rude to callers—and he encouraged Langbourne's roving spirit.

"I'll make a man of you," Bentham kept telling his frisky pet, and Langbourne, more than willing, became a swaggering Puss-in-Boots. No lapping milk from a saucer for him—he sat up at the dinner table and feasted on macaroni—nor any dozing by the fire in the evening. By the light of the moon Langbourne stepped out and ranged the park of Queen's Square Place, serenading and making love to giddy young pussy-cats. So gay a blade did he become that Bentham decided he deserved knighthood and conferred it on him with ceremony. One can

picture the jolly old eccentric royally laying his walking stick on the crouching cat's shoulder and commanding, "Rise, Sir John Langbourne."

Langbourne tolerantly shared the affections of his master, who was fond of all animals, with a strange assortment of other pets. For a time there was a pig which was so delighted at having the jurist tickle his back with his stick that he followed him home, where he squealed so constantly for more attention that he had to be converted into pork chops. Also there was a pet fish Bentham believed he could train to obey. Langbourne was even reconciled to a group of half-tame mice, allowed to scamper through the study, bureau drawers, and across the dining-room table. When the cat was away, the mice might play, but when they became too noisy, Bentham would threaten to summon Sir John, the very mention of whose name was enough to restore order.

So many escapades and scrapes did Langbourne survive, he seemed to be endowed with the proverbial nine lives. Bentham took them for granted. As a boy he had tried to find out if the old saying were true by tossing a cat out the window. It lit unharmed on its feet but cast upward such a reproachful glance that the lad repented of his thoughtless cruelty and ever afterward treated cats with kindness and consideration.

Finally, under the weight of years, Langbourne tired, like Solomon, of the pleasures and vanities of this world and became dignified and sedate. Plainly he was ready to lay down his knightly title and enter the church, so Bentham bestowed a doctor's degree on him and installed him as the Reverend Sir John Langbourne, D.D.

Friends, observing the cat's conspicuous gravity and philosophy, showed great respect for his reverence, and it was supposed that Langbourne was not far from a bishop's miter when a last illness put an end to hopes of fresh honors. At last he departed this life amidst widespread regrets and was gathered to his fathers. Since there was no feline Westminster Abbey, Bentham buried his pet with honors in the garden of the poet Milton.

HINSE OF HINSEFELD

DEFIER OF DOGS

THERE were dogs—many of them—in Sir Walter Scott's household, but he had never cared for cats. The celebrated author of the *Waverley* novels admitted to only a mild liking for "a tolerably conversible cat" that ate a mess of cream with him each morning in a London hotel. Then, on a visit to Naples, Scott dined with the Archbishop of Taranto at his palace. When dinner was announced, several large and beautiful Angoras entered and were introduced as Pantalone, Desdemona, and Otello. They took their places on chairs near the table, were served and ate daintily except for one which declined early courses. "La Signora Desdemona," the butler explained, "will prefer waiting for the roasts." Sir Walter decided that if cats could banquet with archbishops and look at kings, he had been neglecting a notable animal. Forthwith a sleek, black tomcat, named Hinse of Hinsefeld from a character in a German fairy tale, was installed in the Scott home, Abbotsford.

Hinse lorded it over every dog in the house. A book-ladder in the study, on top of which he royally reclined, was a throne, not a refuge. Hinse would descend when the spirit moved him to mount guard, purring, beside his master's footstool. If any dog annoyed him, he clapper-clawed it, and none ever dared retaliate.

Greyhounds, spaniels, and terriers made way for him. Even the huge Scottish deerhound, Maida, acknowledged the sway of the black tom. Hinse, wrote Sir Walter, "keeps Maida in the best possible order and insists on all rights of precedence and scratches with impunity the nose of an animal who would make no bones of a wolf and pull down a red deer without fear or difficulty."

Like the Archbishop's Angoras, Hinse joined his master at meals. When invited, he politely partook of a slice of salmon or other dishes. While Scott was at work, he talked to the cat and his other pets and firmly believed they understood him. A visiting American author, Washington Irving, was inclined to agree when he saw how attentively Hinse listened to Arthurian legends, read aloud by Sir Walter. "Cats are a very mysterious kind of folks," the novelist declared. "There is more passing in their minds than we are aware of. It comes no doubt from their being so familiar with warlocks and witches."

When artists arrived, as they frequently did to paint Scott or his pets, the stately Maida, bored with posing, would howl and run away. Not so Hinse—he recognized himself as a celebrity and saw his duty to posterity. He vastly enjoyed a sitting and was plainly vain of his portrait, hung on a library wall.

All animals loved Sir Walter. On his walks, ponies, donkeys, pigs and chickens would follow him about like dogs, and no exception was the lordly, independent Hinse which joined the master's train. It was during a stroll in the fields that Hinse's fate befell him.

Maida had died and been succeeded by another big stag-

hound, Nimrod. To the newcomer Hinse was not the ruler of the pack but just a cat. Suddenly the ancient dog-and-cat feud flamed up. There was a brief, fierce struggle. Before the master could intervene, Hinse was slain.

Scott sadly wrote a friend: "Alack-a-day! my poor cat Hinse, my acquaintance, and, in some sort, my friend of fifteen years, was nipped at even by that paynim Nimrod. What could I say to him but what Brantôme said to some *ferrailleur* who had been too successful in a duel 'Ah! *mon grand ami, vous avez tué mon autre grand ami.*"

That was both Hinse's epitaph and Nimrod's pardon for an instinctive act. "Ah, my great friend, you have killed my other great friend."

MME. THEOPHILE

PARROT STALKER

UNTIL the green parrot, to be kept for a friend away on a journey, was placed on a perch in the Gautier home, the cat had behaved like a perfect lady with due regard to her position. Her reddish coat with white breast was licked immaculate, her pink nose appreciated perfumes, her blue eyes missed nothing out of order. Did she not preside over the household of Théophile Gautier?

Because the French novelist was unmarried and he and his cat were on such intimate and companionable terms, he called her Madame Théophile. She slept on the foot of the master's bed and sat on the arm of his chair while he wrote. Gravely she strolled through the garden with him. At meals she frequently intercepted a choice morsel on its way from his plate to his mouth.

Graciously Madame Théophile entertained guests. She listened with evident appreciation to singers until voices soared to a high *la*. Then the cat, made nervous by so piercing a note, would leap to the piano top and politely but firmly close the

mouth of the singer with a velvet paw. Never once did she forget her manners and hospitality—till the day when a parrot arrived.

Her master watched her survey the bird with a look of profound meditation. Parrots were strange to her experience, and she seemed to be running through all her notions of natural history to place this creature. Gautier could plainly read her conclusion in her eyes: "Decidedly this is a green chicken."

Madame Théophile jumped from the table from which she had made her observations. She crouched flat on the floor exactly in the attitude of a panther, stalking gazelles drinking at a lake. "The parrot followed the movements of the cat with feverish anxiety," Gautier wrote. "It ruffled its feathers, rattled its chain, lifted one of its feet and shook the claws, and rubbed its beak against the edge of its trough. Instinct told it that the cat was an enemy and meant mischief. The cat's eyes were now fixed on the bird with fascinating intensity, and they said in perfectly intelligible language, which the poor parrot distinctly understood, 'This chicken ought to be good to eat, although it is green.'"

The novelist, ready to interfere at need, saw the cat creep closer and closer, pink nose quivering, eyes half closed, claws unsheathing.

"All in an instant her back took the shape of a bent bow, and with a vigorous and elastic bound she sprang upon the perch. The parrot, seeing its danger, said in a bass voice as grave and deep as M. Prudhomme's own, *'As tu déjeuné, Jacquot?'*" (Have you dined, Jacquot?)

A trumpet blare, the crash of plates, or a pistol shot could not have frightened Madame Théophile more thoroughly. She sprang backward in utter consternation. The parrot inquired further into Jacquot's dinner.

"Et de quoi? Du roti du roi?" (And on what? The king's roast?)

On the visage of the astounded cat, Gautier read her reaction as plainly as if she had spoken: "This is not a bird. It is a gentleman. It talks."

Now the parrot had realized that speech, terrifying its foe, was its surest defense, it shrieked with all its might:

"Quand j'ai bu du vin clairet,
Tout tourne, tout tourne au cabaret."

"When some light wine I have downed,
In the bar all whirls, all whirls around."

After her repulse Madame Théophile fled and hid under the bed, nor would she stir from that refuge all day. Later she ventured one more assault and again she was routed by the talking bird. Thereafter she left it severely alone. Plainly she had decided that it was no chicken but a little man, dressed up in green feathers.

In the Gautier household, other cats, termed the Black and the White Dynasties, reigned after Madame Théophile's day, but none eclipsed the fame given her by a visiting parrot and her master's pen.

BIS

"THE ROTHSCHILD OF CATS"

In a magnificent mansion in Paris, the cat Bis dwelt as master and owner, with a housekeeper of his own to attend him and supply his every want. Pampered with the choicest dainties and petted when he condescended to it, he led a life of spoiled and sumptuous ease.

Surrounding luxury, to which Bis was well accustomed, was provided for him by the will of his owner, a wealthy Parisienne who had lavished on him all her affection and everything that money could buy. During her last years she had been torn by worries that, should Bis survive her, others would never give him the same devoted care and might even turn him out to starve as an alley cat.

Such a catastrophe must never happen to her darling Bis. The lady forestalled it by leaving her considerable fortune to him. When she died, and Bis inherited, he was hailed by the press as "The Rothschild of Cats," since he was handsomely endowed with worldly goods like the rich banking family of that name.

All too often it had happened that when large legacies were

left to an animal, indignant relatives sued and broke the will to claim everything for themselves, but that was not to be Bis's fate. Craftily safeguarding his interest, his owner had named him joint-heir with the city of Paris which was made responsible for the cat's welfare as long as he lived. If the city failed to make certain that Bis enjoyed all his comforts, it would be cut off without a franc.

Frugal city fathers were not letting all that money slip away from them. An official committee was appointed and instructed to call twice a month at the mansion to assure themselves that the cat was well cared for and perfectly contented, and to check that their host was Bis himself in the flesh. There was always the chance that Bis might have died and that the housekeeper, knowing a soft and well-paid job when she had one, might have substituted another cat to carry on for her. Not to be tricked, the suspicious officials took exact measurements of Bis, as carefully as for a Bertillon record, and filed them with a description of all his points in the archives of Paris. It would never do to let the cat and that fortune out of the bag.

Soon Bis took note of those regular visits. While he could not send word to the callers that he was out or indisposed, it struck him that he could at least keep them guessing. It was more fun than catnip to hide when he heard the doorbell and let them hunt. Dignified and disturbed officials in top hats and frock coats scoured the house, peering behind curtains and poking canes or umbrellas under sofas and bed. Plaintively and persuasively they kept calling, "Bis! Bis!" Probably no opera star has heard the traditional call for an encore, "Bis! Bis!" more often nor more happily. After the cat had exploited the situation to the last ounce of pleasure in it, he would emerge from concealment. With what was plainly a grin on his whiskered face, he would lift his shoulders in a Gallic shrug and allow himself to be identified and marked present.

Bis lived on for five years in splendid state, then passed on to whatever rewards a cat hereafter could offer to compare with his earthly bliss. Crediting the Paris treasury with his sizable estate, the cat-calling delegation returned to less exacting duties.

BULGARIAN BELL

BLACK WATCH MASCOT

Often regiments on a campaign pick up stray dogs, for lonely soldiers and lonely dogs crave each other's companionship. A wagging tail, a pat, a scrap of food, and a new mascot trots after the marching column. Cats, though, usually avoid the uniformed strangers, tramping into a city or village, and hide till they have passed.

So it was a surprising event that occurred one day in 1854 when the 42nd Royal Highlanders encamped near the Bulgarian town of Varna. A tall Scot, seated by a fire, felt a furry body rub against bare knees below the kilt of green and blue tartan, so dark that it had given the regiment its name of the Black Watch. The soldier stared down at a thin cat which calmly returned his gaze and mewed ingratiatingly. Purring, she arched her back under stroking by the roughened but gentle hands of the Highlander and his comrades of the first company.

She would not leave after she was fed, but had plainly attached herself for rations.

They called her Bulgarian Bell, and she became as much a member of the regiment as if she had taken the Queen's shilling. A cat might be considered an odd mascot but not by the Black Watch, for Bulgarian Bell's predecessor had been a deer named Donald.

At Varna the Highlanders embarked for the Crimea, where the allied armies of Great Britain and France would lock in bloody conflict with the troops of the Tsar. Along with her regiment sailed Bulgarian Bell, and when the Watch landed and took up the march, the cat was assigned transportation in a soldier's knapsack. Extra burden though she was, she was a highly popular detail because the man who took his turn carrying her was exempt from all other fatigue duties on that day.

Bulgarian Bell bivouacked with her regiment by the shore of Lake Touzla beneath frowning hills where battalions that were the flower of the Russian army were entrenched. Soon smoke wreathed those heights, as cannon thundered the overture for the Battle of Alma. While the Black Watch mustered on the plain below for an attack, an officer strode along the front of the first company, demanding the whereabouts of the mascot cat.

"Here, sir," spoke up a soldier and lifted the flap of his knapsack.

Out popped the head of Bulgarian Bell. Calmly and with marked interest, she looked over the battlefield where shells burst with a roar and the crash of musketry rattled. A sharp order, and bagpipes shrilled the assault. Up against the enemy's position marched the Black Watch with the rest of the Highland Brigade, the Guards, and troops of France. And on with her regiment advanced Bulgarian Bell, probably the first and only mascot cat to go into battle.

Enclosed in the knapsack, she could not see the colors waving proudly over the kilted ranks, nor have sight of the red hackles, those crimson feathers tossing on the bearskins of the

Watch like the fighting crest they were. But she could hear the command, "Charge!" that leveled bayonets and she could feel herself jounced in her carrier, as the Highlanders swept up the slopes. Clamorous in her ears was the din of volleys and, high above them, the skirl of the royal pipes.

After a time there was quiet again and an end to movement. Bulgarian Bell was let out to survey a victorious field from which routed Russians streamed in retreat.

Though the cat went on with her regiment to Balaclava, she did not witness there the gallant but disastrous cavalry charge of the Light Brigade nor the subsequent fighting in which the Scottish infantry took part. It had been decided that her life should not be risked by going into action again, and she had been sent back to the safety of the regimental hospital.

Bulgarian Bell missed active service, the marches and voyages and the evenings beside the campfires with her kilted friends. Pining for them, she sickened and died. Her career had been brief, but she had lived to become a proud tradition of one of the most gallant regiments in any army—the Black Watch.

ATOSSA

CAT AND CANARY

Atossa, the stately Persian, stared upward at Mattias, the canary, while Matthew Arnold watched his two pets with a poet's keen eye. The cat's gaze was a baleful one—such a glare as a merciless monarch of Persia or Rome might have fixed on some unfortunate victim he meant to condemn. Mattias sang blithely on. His cage was a prison but it was also his protection, hung high out of the cat's reach. The canary had grown used to the unwinking regard of that creature crouched below. Perhaps she was admiring him, and the intentions of cats toward canaries were not as malevolent as one might at first have thought.

After a time Atossa would give up her vigil and rival the yellow bird for the affection and attention of their master. Mattias might warble his best, yet she could match him with purring which Arnold called "the sweet voice of Toss." That yellow-feathered creature was only a bird, while Atossa was a pedigreed pussy, named for a Queen of Persia, the daughter of Cyrus and the wife of Cambyses and later of Darius. When she became the proud mother of a kitten, he was called Xerxes.

Arnold mentioned Toss in scores of letters, telling how she stretched out on the floor beside him to let the sun shining through the window bathe the deep, rich, tawny fur of her stomach—how she sat by the fire with him, or slept curled up on the counterpane of his bed; he never woke without her instantly sitting up to regard him solicitously. When he took up his pen, Atossa showed flattering interest in his work, as the cats of writers often do. She would spring upon his lap and sweep her fluffy tail as a blotter over the pages. If Arnold put her down and took no notice of her, she would walk around and around him, purring. Again she would jump into his arms, rub her head and nose against his chin, open her mouth and rap her pretty white teeth against his pen as if to beg, "Put me in your poem."

But Matthew Arnold failed to devote a poem to Atossa in spite of their fond companionship and despite the example of the Italian poet, Domenico Balestrieri whose beloved cat inspired a whole book of poems by himself and his friends, written not only in their own tongue but in Greek, Latin, French and even Arabic. Instead Arnold penned poems to Geist and other dogs of his, and the beautiful Atossa died unsung.

That canary she never had been able to dispose of, either as dinner or a rival, survived her, and it was he that won a tender lament entitled, "Poor Mattias."

But in the end Atossa triumphed after all. She crept into the canary's poem, and the lines about her are among the most famous and most frequently quoted ever written about a cat.

> "Rover, with the good brown head,
> Great Atossa, they are dead,
> Dead, and neither prose nor rhyme
> Tells the praises of their prime.

Thou didst know them old and grey,
Know them in their sad decay."

Remembering the way the cat had gazed at the canary, Arnold wrote on—

"Thou hast seen Atossa sage
Sit for hours beside thy cage;
Thou wouldst chirp, thou foolish bird,
Flutter, chirp--she never stirred!
What were now these toys to her?
Down she sank amid her fur;
Eyed thee with a soul resigned,
And thou deemedst cats were kind!
Cruel, but composed and bland,
Dumb, inscrutable, and grand.
So Tiberius might have sat,
Had Tiberius been a cat."

TOM QUARTZ

GOLD PROSPECTOR

A MINER'S blast blew Tom Quartz sky-high, but he came down with eight out of his proverbial nine lives to spare and lived on for Mark Twain to make him immortal in *Roughing It*.

In a cabin on Jackass Hill in the gold-streaked hills of California, Mark Twain heard the cat's exploits related by his owner, Dick Stoker, and set the story down. While Dick's tales were tall, the great American humorist insisted they were true.

Tom Quartz was described by Stoker as "the remarkablest cat ever I see. He was large gray one of the Tom specie, an' he had more hard, natchral sense than any man in the camp 'n a *power* of dignity—he wouldn't let the Guv'ner of Californy be familiar with him. He never ketched a rat in his life—'peared to be above it. He never cared for nothing but mining."

On prospecting trips Tom would trot along behind the miners for as far as five miles. If gold indications were not good, he would hoist his nose in the air and shove off for home.

But when the ground suited, he would watch the first pan washed. If it showed six or seven grains of gold, he was satis-

fied and would lie down on a coat and snore like a steamboat till a pocket was struck; then he superintended.

Such new-fangled mining methods as sinking a shaft in a quartz ledge seemed plain foolishness to Tom. Still he was a cat with an open mind, and down into the pit he crawled one day to look things over. In the bottom he went to sleep on a gunny sack, and the miners, forgetting he was there, lit the fuse of a powder charge.

A geyser of rocks and dirt roared up into the air. "Right in the dead center of it," Dick declared, "was old Tom Quartz a goin' end over end, an' a snortin' an' a sneezin' an' a clawin' an' a reachin' for things like all possessed."

Tom, said Dick, stretching things a bit, wasn't seen for two and a half minutes. Then in a rain of rubbage he came down ker-whop, battered, blackened and covered with slush. He was very much alive but rightfully indignant, and his owner saw there was no use apologizing. Tom Quartz turned on his heel and marched home.

Although Tom could never afterward be cured of his prejudice against quartz mining, he would sometimes venture to explore a shaft again. Yet the minute he heard a fuse sizzling, he was out of the hole and up a tree in record time.

Mark Twain did not care for dogs, but there were always cats in the Clemens house. "A home without a cat, and a well-fed, well-petted, and properly revered cat, may be a perfect home, perhaps, but how can it prove its title?" he asked in Pudd'nhead Wilson. On his travels he praised Bermuda highly because he found "upwards of a million cats" there but few dogs. When he played billiards, a cat watched him, perched on the corner of the table. He bestowed on his cats such fantastic names as Sour Mash, Apollinaris, Zoroaster, and Blatherskite, "names given them," he explained, "not in an unfriendly spirit, but merely to practice the children in large and difficult styles of pronunciation." And he told his youngsters stories about cats he christened Cataraugus and Catiline.

Though Tom Quartz, the gold miner, was immortal because Mark Twain made him the hero of one of his stories, his renown was increased by a kitten named after him by a President of the United States.

In Theodore Roosevelt's time when the White House was always full of children and pets, there was a cat named Slippers which wandered but always returned for diplomatic dinners to lie in the hall and force the procession to the dining room, led by the President, to detour around him. Slippers' successor was a kitten which cared nothing for state functions; his only purpose in life seemed to be to make that lively household even livelier. He was such an original and independent character that the President promptly made him the namesake of Mark Twain's prospector cat. Tom Quartz II chased the dog Jack around tables and over sofas, and when the forebearing dog tried to flee, the kitten leaped on his hindquarters, and the two went tandem out of the room. After five minutes the kitten stalked solemnly back with an air of immense satisfaction.

Tom Quartz II showed no more respect for high officials than for dogs. President Roosevelt in one of his wonderful letters to his children told them of the occasion when Speaker Joe Cannon of the House of Representatives left the White House after an evening call.

"He spied Mr. Cannon going downstairs, jumped to the conclusion that he was a playmate escaping, and raced after him, suddenly grasping him by the leg the way he does Archie and Quentin when they play hide and seek with him; then loosening his hold he tore downstairs ahead of Mr. Cannon, who eyed him with iron calm and not one particle of surprise."

Certainly Tom Quartz I and II were two of a kind.

CALVIN

CAREER CAT

"Is THIS the residence of Harriet Beecher Stowe, author of *Uncle Tom's Cabin?*"

Often that question was asked by people making pilgrimages to the home of the lady who had written the great antislavery novel. But this time it was a large cat which stood at the front door with a quizzical look that seemed to put the self-same query. As if he had been assured he had come to the right address, he walked in and settled down.

Kind Mrs. Stowe welcomed her guest, obviously a cat of distinction. He was more or less Maltese, exquisitely proportioned and graceful as a young leopard. From his throat to the tips of his feet his fur was white as ermine. The expression on his handsome, whiskered countenance was alert and wise.

The cat's stay might have been permanent, but soon Mrs. Stowe decided to move from New England to Florida. Since she could not take the cat with her, she gave him to another writer, Charles Dudley Warner. The big Maltese found an ideal home and a fond master whose pen would make him one of the most famous of cats.

His gravity won him the name of John Calvin after the Protestant reformer, and so dignified was his presence that he

was never familiarly called by his first name. Yet sometimes he would relax to play with a ball of yarn or chase his tail with hilarious delight.

Calvin was one of the smartest of cats. Being a big cat, he could stand on his hind legs and open all doors which had low, old-fashioned latches. If a room were too cool to suit him, he would turn on the hot-air register. "He could do almost everything but speak," avowed his master, "and you would declare sometimes that you could see a pathetic longing to do that in his intelligent face." To mere mewing Calvin would not condescend, but by mighty and musical purring he expressed his contentment.

No eating in the kitchen for Calvin; he insisted on meals in the dining room where he displayed refined manners. When a fork with a morsel of food was reached down to him on the floor, he would put up a paw and draw it politely to his mouth. Since he had definite tastes and was always aware of the contents of the larder, he would refuse beef if there was turkey in the house and decline turkey if oysters were forthcoming.

He rid the house of rats as a duty, though he did not enjoy it. Mice amused him, but he considered them too small game to be taken seriously. He stalked birds in the garden, mostly those robbing the cherry trees, but he never killed, as some sportsmen do, for the sake of killing, but only to satisfy his appetite. In justification of Calvin and other cats finding birds tasty may be quoted a pointed bit of verse, "The Three Menus":

> "She: The cat has eaten our pet bird;
> He: The wicked beast shall die.
>   Then he resumed his quail on toast
>   And she ate pigeon pie."

Calvin did not care to associate with other cats. When he heard their night-time concerts in the shrubbery, he asked to be let out. A rush and a *pestzt*, and the caterwauling was suddenly quelled, and Calvin, unruffled, would quietly return to his seat by the hearth. Between the Maltese and Warner grew up a close and devoted friendship. The reserved Calvin did not care to be petted but chose to show his own affection delicately, pulling at a coat sleeve until he could touch his master's face with his nose, whereupon he would walk away contented. He would come when called and would wait at the gate for his master's return. "Now when the mistress was absent from home, and at no other time," Warner wrote, "Calvin would come in the morning, when the bell rang, to the head of the bed, put up his forepaws and look into my face, follow me about when I rose, 'assist' at the dressing, and in many purring ways show his fondness, as if he had plainly said, 'I know that she has gone away, but I am here.'"

The fellowship which so often exists between cats and writers was deep and strong with these two. Calvin, his master related, "had a habit of coming to my study in the morning, sitting quietly by my side or on the table for hours, watching the pen run over the paper, occasionally swinging his tail round for a blotter, and then going to sleep among the papers by the inkstand. Or, more rarely, he would watch the writing from a perch on my shoulder. Writing always interested him, and until he understood it, he wanted to hold the pen."

Calvin bore his last illness with calm resignation, purring in grateful response to his master's sympathy. When Warner spoke his name, he looked up with an expression that said, "I understand it, old fellow, but it's no use." His last look was toward the garden he loved. There he was buried under twin hawthorn-trees—one white and the other pink—in a spot where he loved to lie. His master's tribute to him: *Calvin: A Study of Character,* will always rank as one of the great cat biographies.

FOSS

NONSENSE RHYMER'S CAT

"He has many friends, laymen, clerical;
Old Foss is the name of his cat;
His body is perfectly spherical;
He weareth a runcible hat."

So wrote Edward Lear, great English master of nonsense rhymes and drawings, in a verse about himself, "How Pleasant to Meet Mr. Lear." When people met Mr. Lear, they usually also encountered his big, tiger-striped cat, flaunting a comical stump of a tail, and it was pleasant to meet old Foss, too, for he was a character like his master.

Before Foss joined the Lear home, a pleasant villa at San Remo on the Italian Riviera, he somehow had lost part of that tail of his. But he seemed no more embarrassed by the shortage than a Manx, and his master jokingly introduced him as "my cat who has no end of a tail because it has been cut off." As if to make up to him, Lear chose a long Greek word for his name, a word so lengthy and jaw-breaking that nobody could remember it, so only the middle syllable was used to name Foss, and the rest were saved as long as they lasted to christen his kittens.

Foss, a untin,
Foss rampant
Foss Couchant
Foss dansant

Foss was great fun. He prowled about after his master, grinning like a Cheshire cat. Lear mentioned him in many letters and made merry sketches of him, including a series in which he awarded the cat a heraldic blazon picturing Foss *rampant, dormant* and even *dansant.* Perhaps Foss should be given credit for inspiring the famous saga of "The Owl and the Pussy-Cat," though the pussy Lear drew to illustrate his verses had an extra-long tail. But so may Foss have had in his younger days when he would have been more inclined to go to sea with an owl in a beautiful pea-green boat, taking "some honey, and plenty of money wrapped up in a five-pound note."

Lear made even more hilarious drawings of himself than he did of Foss and delighted in caricaturing his own rotund figure and his bushy beard like that of the old man who said:

> "...It is just as I feared.
>   Two Owls and a Hen,
>   Four Larks and a Wren
> Have all built their nest in my beard."

A serious as well as a comic artist, Lear once had given drawing lessons to Queen Victoria, and he was noted especially for his fine paintings of birds. Foss, too, on one occasion seemed to have become a bird-fancier. He was observed keeping vigil beneath the cage of a blackbird which belonged to his master's Italian servant, Giorgio.

"Foss the cat," Lear wrote, "having taken to sit from 5 to 8 A.M. under the cage of George's blackbird, since that very charming animal took to singing, we had very great hope of our cat's aesthetic tendencies, and had expected eventually to hear poor dear Foss warble effusively. But alas! it has been

discovered there is a hole in the lower part of Merlo's cage, and Foss's attention relates to pieces of biscuit falling through."

Lear's friends always asked for Foss when they called, and their letters inquired for his health. A noblewoman sent him a Christmas card. When a hotel was built at San Remo, encroaching on the Lear villa, the author-artist commissioned an architect to plan a new home for him but insisted that it be an exact copy of the old one, since otherwise, as he gravely remarked, Foss would not like it.

The stub-tailed cat lived until nearly his seventeenth birthday, he and his master reaching a vigorous old age together. Lear in his seventy-third year ran a race with Foss from the village to the town of Vintimiglia and proudly recorded that he beat the cat by eight-and-a-half feet. Soon afterwards they sat for their photograph together, but at the last moment Foss jumped from his master's knee, and the picture shows Lear with a surprised expression and an empty hand. It did not matter, since the artist's pen had done more for Foss than any camera could.

Foss was buried in the garden of the new villa, which had been built just like the old one to make him feel at home, mourned by a master who loved him as fondly as the owl did the pussy-cat.

DINAH

ALICE IN WONDERLAND'S CAT

ALICE LIDDELL left her black cat Dinah at home that day a don of Christ Church College, Oxford, took her and her two sisters on a picnic. The don was Charles Lutwidge Dodgson and he taught higher mathematics, but he would sign his pen name of Lewis Carroll to the story he told the three young daughters of the college's dean after they had enjoyed their luncheon on the river bank. There was nothing mathematical or logical in that story—it was all about adventures in Wonderland. And Wonderland was all the more wonderful to Alice because she was its heroine and because she met her cat Dinah there.

The story-teller must have known that Dinah was missed at the picnic when he began describing Alice's conversation with the Mouse that had trouble understanding her, perhaps because it was a French mouse, come over with William the Conqueror. Alice, trying it in its native tongue, burst out with the first sentence in her French book, *"Où est ma chatte?"*

The mouse did understand that all too well and quivered in a tizzy of nerves. Hastily Alice begged its pardon, explaining she'd forgotten that mice never showed any fondness for cats.

"Would you like cats, if you were me?" the Mouse demanded.

"Well, perhaps not," said Alice in a soothing tone; "don't be angry about it. And yet I wish I could show you our cat Dinah. I think you'd take a fancy to cats, if you could only see her. She's such a dear quiet thing, and she sits purring so nicely by the fire, licking her paws and washing her face—and she is such a nice soft thing to nurse—and she's such a capital one for catching mice—oh, I beg your pardon!"

When Alice walked through Wonderland into the Duchess's kitchen, there was Dinah, sitting by the stove and grinning from ear to ear. Why, wondered Alice, did she grin like that?

The Duchess tartly explained:

"It's a Cheshire-Cat, and that's why."

"I didn't know that cats could grin," Alice confessed.

"They all can," said the Duchess, "and most of 'em do."

Certainly Lewis Carroll knew it. In Cheshire, where he was born, they made their celebrated cheeses in the shape of a cat's head, with a broad grin on its face. And naturally when the Cheshire-Cat of Wonderland changed itself into just a huge head in the sky, it still grinned.

When the story was made into a beloved book, Dinah won fame as the original of the Cheshire-Cat. Meanwhile Lewis Carroll was occupied with another cat, official mouser of the college common room of which the don was curator. When that cat became old and ailing he was responsible for ending its suffering, so he consulted eminent surgeons on the gentlest way of putting it to sleep, or as he expressed it in long, professor's words, "terminating its sublunary existence."

But soon there were other picnics and another story for Alice, with Dinah appearing in it right at its start. Through the Looking Glass begins, you remember, with Dinah washing her two kittens, the black one which favored her and the white one which must have taken after its father. Dinah took great pains with the white kitten, holding it down by its ear with one paw, and then with the other paw rubbing its face all over the wrong way, beginning at the nose. Meanwhile the black kitten, finished with earlier, had unwound Alice's ball of yarn in a romp and had to be scolded: "Really Dinah ought to have taught you better manners."

Beyond the looking-glass the kittens turned into the Red and White Queens of chess. Back at home they were kittens again, with Dinah again performing her maternal duty.

"Dinah!" Alice chided her cat. "Do you know you're scrubbing a White Queen? Really it's most disrespectful of you!" And then Alice asked her pet, "Dinah, did you turn into Humpty Dumpty? I think you did—however, you'd better not mention it to your friends just yet, for I'm not sure."

Perhaps Dinah also had a paw in Carroll's short piece about three cats that called on him. He put them up in a portfolio for the night and gave them a breakfast of rat-tail jelly and buttered mice, though they had asked for boiled pelican which wouldn't be good for them. And maybe Dinah's offspring inspired the tale of an overwhelming gift of two hundred and fifty kittens and five hundred pairs of gloves. Carroll wrote he hadn't known what to do until he got the brilliant idea of giving each member of a girls' school a kitten, with two pairs of gloves apiece in case the kittens scratched.

For the children and grownups who love the Alice books, Dinah was indeed a cat of destiny.

NANNY AND HINOKO

LAFCADIO HEARN'S CATS

A NEWSPAPERMAN sauntering toward his boarding house in a dingy quarter of New Orleans, halted abruptly in mid-step. Lafcadio Hearn was blind in one eve and his sight weakened in the other from constant reading, but he could make out a scene down the street well enough to be disquieted and alarmed.

A husky, heavy-set man was striding out of a house, carrying a pail of water and clutching an armful of kittens. Before the watcher could stir the fellow set the pail on the curb and began plunging each little creature under water. Perhaps kittens that could not be cared for had to be mercifully disposed of but never with such callous brutality.

Hearn was small and slight, yet he charged toward the big man in a white-hot rage. Cruelty to animals was unforgivable, and he would kill that scoundrel.

He arrived too late to get his hands on the executioner, for the man turned without even pausing to see if any of his victims still were struggling. and swaggered back into the house,

slamming the door. But there might still be time to save the kittens, and Hearn rushed for the pail in desperate haste.

Quick as he was, another rescuer was faster. The mother cat flashed over a fence like an arrow and started desperately trying to fish her offspring out of the water. She recognized that this human, who knelt on the pavement helping her, was a friend and let him pull out the tiny, drenched bodies. There was still a spark of life in one of them—all the rest were drowned. Hearn hurried home with the living one and as soon as his Irish landlady, Mrs. Courtney, had warmed it before the fire, the writer dried it gently with soft rags. Mewing feebly, it came back to life, and Hearn put it to bed on a cushion in a corner of the dining room.

Nanny was the name he gave his pet, a sprightly gray tabby. She grew in devotion and wisdom and soon she was waiting to meet him at the door when he came home from work.

She would arch her back to be rubbed and purr in contentment. At meal times she would jump to her special chair beside his, sitting there decorously while he ate, and daintily accepting tidbits from his hand. On Fridays he always ordered a special fish dish cooked for her as a treat.

Hearn's affection for Nanny inspired him to write pieces about cats, and in his charming style he made translations from the French about the cats of Pierre Loti and De Maupassant, and Zola's two, named Frances and Catherine. He also penned an amusing yarn about a Belgian who tried to train cats on the carrier-pigeon plan. Each trainee was lapped in luxury in its own home for a time and then was shifted to a different domicile where clotted cream, warm corners, and all comforts were denied. The theory was that when the cats were released, they would speed back to their own pleasant homes, carrying messages which had been tied around their necks. The freed cats did depart in haste, but they lingered so long on the way home to dally and serenade with fence-top friends that the messages would have arrived sooner by oxcart.

For five years Nanny was Hearn's loving companion. Then he transferred to New York and, unable to take her, left her in care of his landlady. Later on Mrs. Courtney was forced by reduced circumstances to move, and since there was an Irish superstition that it was bad luck to take a cat to a new address, Nanny was left behind. But a kind-hearted niece returned to the vacant house every day to solace Nanny's loneliness and feed her until the tabby's death.

Nanny was gone and perhaps forgotten by the master who had loved her, but another cat would come into his life in almost the same way Nanny had. Hearn, sensitive and eccentric, ill at ease in the United States, fled to Japan. There he married a Japanese lady of samurai rank and found happiness teaching school and writing books about his adopted country. One day Hearn's wife, strolling along the shore of a lake, caught a group of boys in the act of drowning a black cat. She would not listen when they shouted that it was one of those devil cats that dance on roofs at night with scarves wound round their heads. Scolding the superstitious youngsters, she snatched their victim and carried it home where she told her husband its story.

"O pity! Cruel boys!" Hearn moaned. He took the little cat in his arms and warmed it under his shirt against his skin. The name he gave it was Hinoko, meaning spark, because its eyes glowed like live coals.

Hinoko lived a happy life in the Hearn home in amity with another pet, an *uguisu*, a tiny bird the Japanese believe is holy. They say it professes Buddhism because when it sings it warbles the sacred name over and over again. Perhaps it was a prayer for its friend, Hinoko, the *uguisu* seemed to be saying, since cats, along with snakes, are barred from paradise because they were the only two creatures which did not weep for the death of Buddha.

PETER

COMIC MODEL

Nobody minded Cordelia having seven kittens. It was where she put them to bed that caused consternation in the Wain household. The mother cat picked Mrs. Wain's fur-lined bonnet as a nursery for part of her litter and the lady's best muff for the rest.

Louis Wain, son of the house—just nineteen and later to become a celebrated English illustrator—chose a black kitten, tucked snugly into one end of the muff, for his own. The little thing's coat was inky except for a white muzzle and cravat that made him appear all ready to step out for the evening in a full-dress suit. As soon as he opened his eyes, his look was knowing and twinkling, and his waving tail as he strolled about was "as expressive as an orator's arm." While Louis was studying what name to give him, a rooster in the yard crowed loudly. Hadn't Peter the Apostle denied his Lord thrice before the cock crowed? Let the kitten be called Peter then. Perhaps he would display the fidelity of St. Peter before and after he gave way under stress at Gethsemane.

Louis, fond of animals, started training Peter, and though

few cats will bother to learn tricks, Peter was the aptest of scholars. On command he would lie down and play dead, sit up with spectacles on his nose, or mew silent meows. When he wanted to come in the front door, he lifted a corner of the doormat and let it fall with a whack, repeating until he was admitted. His best trick was saying his prayers erect on his hind quarters, with paws folded over his face. Without orders, Peter would pray every evening, and that was an accomplishment which would stand him in good stead later on one night.

Peter was always striking amusing poses. Once while he was still a kitten he heard a scurrying behind a partition and scratched a hole through to find a rat. It was not much smaller than he, but he conquered it in a mighty tussle and proudly presented it as a trophy to his master. Louis watched him stalk back to the hole, crouch before it and mew defiantly, daring more rats to come out and fight. At last, his challenge unanswered, it dawned on Peter that he was using poor tactics, and he looked up at his master with a comical expression that fairly demanded to be drawn.

Louis wrote and illustrated a story about Peter which a magazine promptly accepted. Then and there began their notable success as artist and model. Hundreds of cats scampered from the Wain pen to cavort on the pages of English magazines. Gay toms partnering pretty pussies at dances. Mittened and mufflered cats in snowball fights, or bringing in the Yule log. Feline suffragettes addressing a cats' rights meeting with tomcats in the back row, sniffing and indignantly twirling their whiskers. Peter was always the chief model, but other cats in the home posed, too, as did the pets of noblewomen, aristocratic Persians, Angoras, and Chinchillas which sat to Wain for their portraits in oils.

Peter grinned, gamboled or rode a motorbike on calendars and postcards, to the delight of cat-lovers, especially children. He was often a feature of Wain's Annual, devoted to pictures and stories of pussies. But Peter for all his faithful posing was something of a scamp and deeply disgraced himself once during one of the trips on which he always accompanied his master through the British Isles. In a boarding house he invaded the room of a woman guest at night and stole her false teeth from the bedside table. Peter's appearance, carrying the dental plate in his mouth, was a hilarious sight—he seemed to be out-grinning Alice in Wonderland's Cheshire-Cat—but the owner of the teeth was not amused. She insisted on the immediate ousting of Peter and Wain from the boarding house.

And unfortunately Peter had a bad case of wanderlust. He ran away in London, picking fights with other toms and seeking adventures. When he did not return, Wain ran an advertisement in newspapers.

"COME BACK, PETER. Lost, stolen, strayed, or poisoned, a white and black cat called Peter, who left his friends Monday afternoon last. Round his neck he wore a blue ribbon, with the word Peter embroidered upon it in red silk. Before retiring to rest he always says his prayers. Dead or alive, a reward of Two Pounds is offered to anyone who will restore him to his mourning friends."

The advertisement brought the runaway home safe, but again he strayed. This time he was snatched up by a shabby man who held him for ransom for a while. When the thief could not locate the cat's owner, Peter was in mortal danger of being disposed of as incriminating evidence. In the nick of time he performed one of his tricks, and his captor, happening to be an animal showman, was overjoyed. He was building an act around Peter, when Wain discovered his pet and redeemed him from bondage.

A third time Peter skipped out, and Wain searched high and low for him in vain. At the end of a long patrol through London streets, the artist glanced up at a window. Behind the drawn shade of a lighted room he saw the silhouette of a cat sitting up, nose raised devoutly, front paws pressed together. It was bedtime, and Peter was saying his prayers.

After that rescue Peter behaved and stayed home. His congenial company convinced his master that people who keep cats don't suffer from petty ailments and have better dispositions. "I have often felt the benefit after a long spell of mental effort, of having my cats sitting across my shoulders, or of an hour's chat with Peter," Wain wrote.

Surely it was Peter's influence that persuaded Louis Wain to organize a supper for the cats-meat men of London and to take the presidency of the National Cat Club of England.

Peter's biography, *The Cat o' One Tail*, was written by Charles Morley and illustrated by Peter's proprietor.

Best of all, it was Wain's pen and Peter's charm that did much to raise cats from the low esteem in which they long had been held in England, a horse and dog country, and make them prized as pets and beloved as friends.

BLANCHE AND CHINOISE

EAST MEETS WEST

BUGLES blew action stations aboard the French warship, as a Chinese junk under cover of fog slipped up alongside to launch a furious attack. That daring pirate craft had maneuvered close enough to board, when the Frenchman's blazing guns sank her to the bottom of the China sea, and only one boarder, a cat, gained the warship's decks with an agile leap.

The terrified, trembling creature sought refuge in the cabin of Lieutenant Julien Viaud, widely known by his pen name of Pierre Loti as the author of romantic tales of his voyages on the seven seas and adventures in ports from Tahiti to Iceland. The naval officer tried to put the cat out, but her yellow eyes besought him with such an intense, imploring, human gaze that he let her stay. She was an appealing little thing—this Chinoise, this Chinese cat—scrawny from a meager diet that probably had amounted to no more than a fish head now and then and a bit of boiled rice. Tawny as a wild hare and spotted like a leopard, breast and muzzle white, her ears the batlike, exaggerated ones of the Oriental cat, Chinoise's very ugliness was piquant. Loti fed her and stroked her head affectionately.

When the ship made a Chinese port, Loti clapped his hands and ordered, "Off with you, little puss!" but she would not go, and his heart would not let him force her. During the voyage home, he came to cherish her. Somehow she seemed like a little princess, changed into a cat by a wicked witch. Chinoise in turn had given her devotion to Loti, for he had a way with cats, treating them so that they felt: Here is a man who understands us, who knows how to touch us, who is among our friends and to whose petting he can graciously condescend.

Yet Loti was troubled as he approached his home in France. Another cat was awaiting him there—the imperious Moumette (pussy) Blanche, a beautiful Angora whose fur was snowy white except for a black patch over her brow, worn like a chic bonnet, a jet cloak over her shoulders, and a superior sable tail. Spoiled and capricious, Blanche had reigned five years over the household without a rival. She boasted her own visiting cards which read: *Madame Moumette Blanche. Première chatte. Chez M. Pierre Loti.*

The French officer dreaded introducing the Oriental cat into his home where Blanche presided. His fears were realized by a battle royal between the jealous "first cat" and the newcomer. Loti, hastily summoned to the seat of war, the kitchen, was almost deafened by strident, feline shrieks. He saw a whirling ball of white and yellow fur and claws bounding about amid crashing plates and glasses. Only by pouring water over the antagonists was he able to chill their ardor for mortal combat and separate the two grappled cats, tattered and torn.

They never fought again. At first Blanche tolerated the other *moumette* disdainfully, realizing that she must be resigned to her presence since she belonged to the master. Gradually came a growing cordiality which warmed into a beautiful friendship. The two tidied each other's coats with licking tongues—basked side by side in the chimney corner, watching the leaping flames—slept curled up together in a chair—ate from the same dish. When Loti dined, they sat at his right and left. Allied, they repelled invasion of the garden by all other cats except for two toms of their choice. And at the same time they became mothers of a kitten apiece.

For Chinoise, because she had been transplanted to a strange land, Loti built a little pagoda in his garden, and within its musk-and-sandlewood-scented interior the tawny cat felt at home. Always the two cats eagerly awaited the sailor-author when he returned from cruises. When Chinoise died, the grieving Blanche did not long survive her. Loti lovingly wrote their story in his *The Book of Pity and of Death* for his young son, Samuel, "when he knows how to read."

CRISTOBAL COLON

TROPHY FROM THE SPANIARDS

BIG naval guns thundered as the Spanish fleet steamed out of the harbor of Santiago, Cuba. On that July day of 1898, Admiral Cervera had determined that he would no longer submit to being bottled up on port. He would sink the blockading American Navy or fight his way through and sail back to Spain.

Below decks in the Spanish cruiser, *Cristobal Colon*, a gray tabby, cringed in terror. She was seagoing, a veteran ship's cat, and had heard the guns fire in target practice, but never before had she known the dreadful, clanging explosions of hostile shells raining down on her floating home. Her sailor friends, manning the batteries and stoking the white-hot fires in the engine room, could spare no time to comfort her.

A hail of American steel, avenging the battleship *Maine*, blown up in Havana harbor the previous February with the loss of two hundred and sixty-eight lives, smashed into the Spanish squadron. Three of its vessels, smoke and flame pouring from them, ran ashore. But the cruiser with the gray tabby aboard escaped to flee down the coast in a running fight. The *Oregon* and the *Brooklyn* pursued her hotly, guns of their forward tur-

rets pounding her mercilessly. No more than a wreck ready to sink was the *Cristobal Colon* when the American ships overtook her, and seamen from the *Oregon* boarded to rescue the wounded. The Spanish fleet was destroyed, and the way clear for our Army to complete the conquest of Cuba and liberate the island from the yoke of Spain.

One of those saved from the sinking Spaniard was the tabby cat, terrified but unhurt. Sailors gave her to Captain Clark of the *Oregon*. He named her Cristobal Colon after her ship and sent her to his brother in Michigan to keep for him until he was assigned to shore duty.

Now began a triumphal journey for Cristobal. Tacked to her traveling basket was a placard which read:

TO GOOD AMERICANS

"Treat me kindly and give me food, as I am a prisoner of war from the *Cristobal Colon*, being forwarded by my captors, the crew of the *Oregon*, to their gallant commander, Captain Charles E. Clark, whose brave efforts forced the *Colon* to surrender July 3, 1898."

Crowds gathered at stations to welcome Cristobal. She was photographed and "interviewed," and some reporters were so enthusiastic that they declared she had been Admiral Cervera's own pet.

After she was installed in her new home, visitors kept coming to see her, and soon it became plain that she was such a famous cat that she could not retire to seclusion. She graciously acted as a patroness for a military tea given to raise funds for an Indianapolis kindergarten, and her charming manners won hearts and more praise from the press, for she never failed to advance to the front of her enclosure and put her paws up to greet guests.

Chicago next requested a personal appearance by Cristobal. Since that city was the home of many of the crew of the *Oregon*, she could not refuse. At a number of large gatherings, she received visitors as she reclined in a basket on a cushion of red and yellow, the colors of Spain. In appreciation of her service as a war trophy, she was presented with a medal.

At last battle fatigue and the strain of her travels and appearances, proved too much for Cristobal. She returned home worn out and laid down the last of her nine lives.

AGRIPPINA

FIRESIDE SPHINX

SHE was as haughty as the Roman empress for whom she was named, and the spirit of all the arrogant cats of history looked out from her yellow eyes. Yet to Agrippina's owner, Agnes Repplier, the essayist, the very indifference of cats was honest, and their charm lay in what they held back, rather than what they gave.

Agrippina, jet-black with a white face, breast, and forelegs, refused to fetch slippers or make herself of any service--such errands were for dogs. She was choosy about her food, picking out the biscuits she liked at the grocer's and insisting on cream and sugar on her morning oatmeal. But in spite of her airs, she gave token that she returned the affection lavished on her. When Miss Repplier left the room, Agrippina followed mewing, and as if realizing her duty as the pet of an author, she took her post on the writing table. She might fall asleep, but there she lay, a living inspiration for the graceful essays that flowed from her mistress's pen and for *The Fire-side Sphinx* and other fascinating books about cats.

Agrippina could relax from her imperial dignity and be gay

as well as grave. She displayed a lively curiosity about closets, drawers, and noises, while from the safety of the window sill she taunted passing terriers till they were frantic. When Harrison Morris was a guest, Agrippina always chose his lap as her throne, but hers was a highly original method of reaching it. She would climb to the mantelpiece, catapult herself six feet to a bookcase top, hang from a broad-framed picture, and then land on Morris, seated on the sofa below. He scolded her for acting like a stable-born cat but was immensely flattered by her liking.

Miss Repplier preferred spinsterhood, but not so Agrippina. Ignoring lectures on its advantages, she demanded to be let out evenings for trysts with a black alley cat. When she bore a kitten, it was inevitably named Claudius Nero after the son of the empress whose namesake she was. Though a basket in the kitchen had been designated as the nursery, the mother cat would have none of it. A kitten, she indicated, should be quartered in a more sheltered spot where it would not be handled too often. Agrippina selected the bedroom closet, carried Claudius Nero upstairs and settled him there. Bowing to the imperial edict, Miss Repplier laid a rug on the closet floor and removed the clothes and the door from its hinges for the greater convenience of the royal family.

All too short are the lives of cats, and Agrippina's allotted span was unwontedly brief. Dedicating *The Fireside Sphinx* to her pet and the memory of their fond companionship, Agnes Repplier made a moving prayer that Agrippina find a sunny corner of the Elysian Fields in which to drowse and play in the company of a little band of cats, whose names are as imperishable as their masters'.

"Into this august assembly, into this sacred circle, I fain in moments of temerity would introduce a little shade who stole too soon from the warm sun, and from the simple joys of life. She was dearly loved and early lost, and the scanty honors years of toil have brought me I lay at her soft feet for the entrance fee. May Hodge and Hinse champion her cause with the Immortals for the sake of the unfaltering love I have ever borne their masters, and may her grace and beauty win for her what my poor pen is powerless to attain. Dear little ghost, whose memory has never faded from my heart, accept this book, dedicated to thee, and to all thy cherished race. Sleep sweetly in fields of asphodel, and waken, as of old, to stretch thy languid length and purr soft contentment to the skies."

MIKE

BRITISH MUSEUM GUARDIAN

FORTY centuries looked down on the kitten Mike, a tiny, furry bundle in a grown cat's mouth, that day in 1908 when he made his entrance into the Egyptian Room of London's famous British Museum. Around and about Mike and his carrier, a large cat named Black Jack, stood images of the feline deities and sacred cats of ancient Egypt. There towered statues of Bast, the cat goddess, and Sekhmet, cat-headed deity of war. Yonder crouched a lion-bodied Sphinx, staring with stony eyes. Cases displayed mummies of cats which might have been ancestors of the two modern ones which had just entered.

Surroundings mirroring the cat-worship of a mighty past, the grown cat seemed to have calculated, would assure a warm reception for the portable kitten and especially for himself.

Black Jack, whose inky coat was lightened by a white chest and paws, was returning from exile and disgrace. Long a Museum inmate, he had betrayed his trust one night in the Library by sharpening his claws on the backs of bound newspaper volumes, leaving them in tatters. Now he was risking a return.

He marched straight up to Sir E. A. Wallis Budge, Keeper of Egyptian and Assyrian Antiquities, who better than any other should be aware of the reverence due cats. Down at Budge's feet he laid his burden, the striped kitten.

Here, he intimated, was his successor. The Keeper could assume if he liked that this was one of Black Jack's offspring, being launched on a career, or even a homeless waif on which he had taken pity. Immediate forebears did not matter. Perhaps the kitten was a lineal descendant of the divine Bast. How could an Egyptologist dare refuse him sanctuary?

Sir Wallis took up the little creature in his arms. Satisfied, Black Jack stalked out. Personally he had no further need of the Museum, since he had found a comfortable home with two staff members who had cared for him during his banishment.

Quickly the kitten, given the name Mike, grew in size and authority. Waitresses in the Museum restaurant served him luncheon. Though Budge's house was open to him, Mike found a handier and more informal home in the quarters of one of the gate-keepers. He ousted mice and dogs which failed to realize that the British Museum was for cats and humans only, and when he tackled dogs, he seemed to swell to twice his size and attacked with fury.

After another house cat taught him to hunt pigeons, Mike acted as if he had taken note of time-honored precedent depicted in paintings showing hunting cats of the Pharaohs retrieving waterfowl. As if the blood of such ancestors ran strong in his veins, he would creep close to the pigeons and point them. A pair of the dumfounded birds, unable to stir, would be seized by Mike and his companion and gently carried to the gate-keeper, who traded the cats a slice of beef and a saucer of milk for them and then set their unharmed prey free. Exchanging raw pigeon for cooked meat was Mike's idea of a good swap.

He was finicky about his fish, too, and would eat only certain varieties. But even during the lean war years his tastes were catered to, and he lived better than most Britons.

Like the Museum, Mike was an institution. No visitors dared treat him with familiarity. Ladies who playfully poked parasols at him shrank back from the indignant growl, and swift claws ripped gloves on hands that ventured to stroke him. Only from Sir Wallis Budge and the gate-keeper, his sponsors and friends, would he tolerate intimacy.

For eighteen years Mike stood guard, then passed on to his reward. Though they did not make a mummy of him and bury him in a model of a pyramid, as, perhaps, a cat so intimate with the Egyptian Room deserved, modern honors were heaped on his memory. Newspapers paid him tribute and Sir Wallis wrote his biography, while another staff member penned an epitaph ending:

> "Old Mike! Farewell! We all regret you,
> Although you would not let us pet you;
> Of cats the wisest, oldest, best cat,
> This be your motto—Requiescat!"

FEATHERS

KITTEN ON THE KEYS

THE lovely, lively kitten called Feathers explored her home. She leaped to a window sill and gazed out at New York City traffic. Nonchalantly she strolled along the backs of sofas. Curiosity killed a cat, they say, but so far it had done Feathers no harm, and she kept right on investigating.

Yonder she saw a stretch of gleaming, white ivory, with black ridges along it at intervals. That should make a fascinating promenade. In a graceful, soaring arc from a chair, Feathers landed squarely on the piano keyboard. There was a sudden, jangling noise, and the kitten crouched, rigid, on the yielding ivory.

It had sounded like the screech of another pussy, hidden inside this rosewood box. Feathers dared it to come out, stalking from one end of the keyboard to the other and producing an exotic succession of tones. She pounced, then dashed wildly from treble to bass. The savage, dissonant chords she struck sounded to her listening master, Carl Van Vechten, author and music critic, like Ornstein's *Wild Men's Dance*.

Feathers was finally convinced there was no other cat in

the box. She herself was making this music and she liked it. Indeed she had joined a notable company of piano-playing cats whose capers on the instrument inspired Scarlatti's *The Cat's Fugue*, often performed by Liszt; Chopin's *Valse Brillante*, and Confrey's rollicking ragtime, *Kitten on the Keys*.

Of the Persian Queen breed, Feathers, a tortoise-shell and white smoke tabby, was blessed with beauty—no disadvantage to a female concert artist. Like all her kind, she preferred giving her concerts at night, but not for her were vocal efforts on a back fence which drew barrages of shoes instead of applause. As a piano virtuoso, Feathers stuck to her instrument. All too often she woke her master at 2 A.M., rippling prodigious scales up and down the keyboard. While Van Vechten, being a music critic, could appreciate her playing, he was no composer to record it for posterity. He was only an author, and he played on an instrument called the typewriter.

Its monotonous, unmusical clicking annoyed Feathers almost as much as the airplanes she growled at when they roared overhead through the New York sky. Worse, that machine took away attention that was Feathers' due. She could not know that on it was being written a book which would become a classic of cat lore, *The Tiger in the House*. A photograph of her would be its frontispiece, and she and her musicianship would be features of the chapter, "The Cat in Music." And it would enroll her among the illustrious cats of all time.

But how could celebrity among strangers compare with the caresses of a master here and now? This man, always so busy writing, could render Feathers the love and homage that were her right, if only he put his mind to it instead of on that book. Feathers sat and gazed impatiently and reproachfully at him as he wrote. When he dropped sheets of manuscript on the floor, she scratched at them jealously and she picked her way scornfully among the heaps of reference works he was using volumes and pictures which he would present to the Yale University Library to form a notable collection of "Puss in Books."

The book had been started when Feathers was a kitten, and during the fourteen months of its writing she had grown up. Though she had had her music to solace her, it was not enough.

At last the final page was drawn from the typewriter. The master pushed back his chair and looked up. Joyfully Feathers leaped into his lap and settled down to contented sleep. Being in a book was well enough, but here on the warmth of her master's knees was where she belonged.

TOMMY POSTOFFICE

HE HELD UP THE MALL

OUT tumbled a kitten in a cascade of letters and packages, as a mail-pouch was emptied on the sorting table of the Hartford, Connecticut, post office. Mailmen bent over the bit of black fur, limp and nearly smothered but not quite dead. That pouch had been packed full in New York twelve hours before, and it was a miracle that there was still any life in the kitten.

Mercy held up the distribution of United States mail, while a postman ran to warm milk. Meanwhile Koko, the office spaniel, leaped upon the table to lick the small body with a tender tongue, until the kitten stirred and revived enough to take the milk from a nippled bottle. Gazing up at his rescuers, the kitten weakly purred his thanks and made himself at home.

Tracing him back to the branch where he had been mailed, the Hartford postmen learned the kitten's name was Tommy Postoffice. His mother had put him to bed in a spare pouch and gone to fetch her other four kittens when the sack was snatched up, filled and shipped north. Yes, New York would be glad to have Tommy carry on his family traditions as the Hartford office cat, so Tommy was installed forthwith. Since he had not arrived as official mail and so should not have traveled free, they stuck a two-cent stamp on Tommy's black brow and a one-cent one on the white tip of his tail which he waved, flaunting the green profile of Ben Franklin, the first American Postmaster General, like a banner.

Tommy Postoffice grew up into a handsome cat, his black coat and white face, breast, and stockings always kept immaculate. The staff chipped in regularly for his milk, adding tidbits from their lunches. Nor was Tommy selfishly concerned with his own appetite only, for if the superintendent were too busy to eat on time and looked hungry, the cat would jump on his desk and offer him a fat mouse. He not only did his duty as a mouser splendidly but seemed well aware that he was a postal employee, for he would sometimes take his stand at the general delivery window and stamp each letter with his paw before it was passed out.

Only once was he false to his trust. Postmen, who caught him rolling delightedly in the contents of a package he had torn open, forgave him his crime and made good the loss, when they understood the temptation had been more than Tommy could withstand—the package was full of catnip. Friends of his outside the office heard the story, and thereafter letters, stuffed with catnip and directed personally to Tommy Postoffice, kept arriving and were duly delivered to the addressee.

Considering the press of his work, Tommy must have thought he needed an assistant and besides he was mindful of his duty as a father, as some tomcats are. One day he walked into the station, carrying a black-and-white kitten, his very image, by the scruff of the neck, and installed his son as a member of the staff.

Clever Tommy willingly learned tricks taught him by his

postmen pals. He shook hands, played dead, sang for his dinner and ate it politely with a napkin around his neck. His best accomplishment was sitting up on his haunches and engaging in a spirited boxing bout with a friend, claws sheathed like a good sportsman. The office, proud of its talented cat, entered him in the Hartford cat show, where Tommy, not a whit abashed by all the pedigreed Angoras and blue Maltese, took the blue ribbon for general intelligence before an enthusiastic cheering-section of gray-coated letter-carriers. Incautiously, Tommy was left in his cage overnight next to that of a prize-winning tortoise-shell pussy. Evidently that haughty neighbor must have insulted him by calling him a common post office cat, or mews to that effect, for the next morning both cages were found broken open and the prize tortoise-shell badly beaten up by the indignant Tommy.

Though Tommy could more than hold his own with other cats or hostile dogs, a human enemy and dreadful fate threatened him when his admirer, the station engineer, went on leave and was temporarily replaced by a surly, evil-tempered fellow. The substitute hated cats and drove Tommy from the furnace room, but Tommy strolled back one night along the top of a partition and when he saw the new man open his lunch box, he dropped on his shoulder to beg a morsel just as he often had done with Dan, the engineer.

Yelling and cursing, the startled man grabbed Tommy Post-office and in a fit of wild rage hurled him into the boiler ashpit, glowing with red-hot coals.

Tommy's shrieks of anguish brought rescuers rushing, as the brutal scoundrel ran, never to dare return. Poor Tommy had sprung from the pit and lay writhing in agony on the floor, all his fur and claws and part of his tail burned off, the pads of his paws like scorched stumps. Never was any hurt creature given fonder care. Postmen swathed him in oiled bandages, nursing him day and night and coaxing him to eat, until at last he managed to take a little milk. Somehow he finally recovered; his coat and whiskers grew in again, and, though his good looks were gone, he became his old, lively self. During his convalescence, Tommy's kitten took over his duties and cheered his father's friends by proving to be a perfect copycat.

Still it was Tommy Senior's right to receive a distinguished visitor when Owney, the famous post office dog, arrived by train and mail wagon to pay his respects at Hartford, as he did at post offices all over the United States and throughout the world. At first Tommy was disposed to give battle to the strange dog, but Owney trotted up to play, and the gay jangling of the decorations and tags he carried on his special harness as testimonials of his travels inspired a more hospitable mood in Tommy. The dog and the cat amicably ate dinner from the same dish, and to grinning postmen they seemed to be exchanging stories, Owney spinning yarns of his globe-trotting and Tommy coming back with some of his local exploits. "Every animal to his taste," they seemed to be agreeing. Dogs are often wanderers, while cats are usually homebodies. "After all," they appeared to be telling each other, "we both work for the same grand old institution, Uncle Sam's postal service."

In his lifetime a fine biography of Tommy Postoffice was written by Gabrielle E. Jackson, and today after forty-five years he is warmly remembered in the Hartford office where he caught mice and helped handle the mail.

TAMA-CHAN

JAPANESE WINDOW DRESSING

THE cat in the window of the Tokyo music store made a fascinating display, playing up to the watching crowd outside. He blinked and purred so loudly he could be heard through the glass and capered and leaped about in pursuit of imaginary butterflies. Among the spectators, an American traveler and bookman, Vincent Starrett, saw that this creature was nothing like the familiar mousers, dozing among the canned goods in grocery windows back home. This indeed was a cat with a mission, a mission which did not include mice.

For the cat Tama-Chan was cavorting in front of a background of samisens—long-necked, three-stringed Japanese banjos with square, skin-covered bodies. Though the strings were not catgut but made of sheep intestines, the drumheads certainly were cat skins—two to a samisen—and Tama-Chan sooner or later was marked for doom. Someday his hide, too, would serve as the sounding base for chords daintily swept by the fingers of Japanese girls. His pelt was destined literally to be the stake in what Americans would call a skin game.

Gaily unsuspecting, Tama-Chan kept acting as an animated window display, attracting large daily audiences. Business poured into the shop, and each mail brought a flood of fan let-

ters. The store proprietor, Tomijuro Kinnazawa, realized that turning this living advertisement of his wares into a samisen would be not only the deed of an ingrate but poor public relations as well, so he reprieved Tama-Chan's death sentence and started a postal savings account in his pet's name. Tama-Chan became the wealthiest cat in Tokyo, with a fortune amounting to 1000 yen.

Immensely popular, Tama-Chan lived out his natural span. When he died, friends and admirers sent eighty wreaths and contributed 400 yen to various charities for the repose of his spirit. Funeral services, costing the Kinnazawa family 4000 yen, were conducted by the Lord Abbot of Zojo Temple, assisted by seventy priests, and attended by a throng of mourners.

Tama-Chan was buried in the cemetery of Taishen Temple, appropriately near the tomb of the man who perfected the samisen, after the custom of the Japanese, who have given ceremonious burial to many thousand beloved household pets—cats, dogs, birds, insects, and fish—beneath tombstones or bronze monuments. Incense is burned in their memory, and every September 21 a Buddhist mass is celebrated in their honor.

In the home of the Kinnazawas a miniature shrine was dedicated to Tama-Chan, and there every morning a bowl of rice was offered so that through him the spirits of all cats, which gave their lives to make music resound from samisens, might be propitiated. A Tama-Chan II was installed in the shop, but he never equaled the lively charm and drawing power of the first of the name.

To this day you will see porcelain "beckoning cats" shown in the windows of Japanese merchants to bring good luck and customers, as Tama-Chan did.

NAPOLEON

WEATHER PROPHET

FOR more than forty days and forty nights it had not rained, and Baltimore, parched and suffering in that long drought of 1930, envied Noah. The Weather Bureau promised no relief. "Continued Dry" was still the bitter forecast.

In the office of the *Baltimore Sun* a telephone rang, and a woman's voice announced there would be rain within twenty-four hours. How did she know? tolerantly demanded a desk man. Why, Napoleon had foretold it, and he never failed, confidently stated Mrs. Fannie de Shields. No, she had not been in touch with the late Emperor of France via the spirit world.

Napoleon was her cat, a beautiful, pure-white, short-haired Persian, nine years old. She had found him in his predicting position: crouched on his stomach with his head down between his front paws as if he were bothered with a headache. When Nappy took that pose, it meant a change of weather, and you could always count on it.

The newspaperman, member of a skeptical profession used to crackpots, muttered thanks and rang off. But before the twenty-four hours were up, the drought was broken. It rained buckets. It rained, as the saying goes, cats and dogs, especially cats—to give Napoleon due credit.

Napoleon's reputation was made. Reporters and photographers flocked to his home. Mrs. de Shields had to chase, catch and hold him for pictures and interviews, since Napoleon disliked men, and unless his publicity came through newspaperwomen, he could do without it. Speaking for him, his proud mistress related that Nappy had possessed his prophetic powers since kittenhood. When he reclined on his side as cats usually do, the weather would remain as it was, but once he assumed his predicting position, bottom dollars or last dimes could be bet on some change short of a complete shift of climate.

Moved to predict, up would spring Napoleon to the top of a white marble table in the hall. Down went head between front paws. There the cat would stay, glancing up now and then to see whether he was observed by the family. It might be hours, but he would not budge until he was certain that his posture had been checked and his duty as a seer performed.

Other cats have been known to foretell weather changes by their actions, but Napoleon was Old Reliable in that role. Except when he needed teeth pulled or was otherwise out of sorts, he never missed. More than a few times he flatly contradicted the officials of the Weather Bureau and turned their faces red, while his serene and whiskered countenance remained white.

"Tell the Government to buy that cat and get rid of the weather forecaster," urged one of Nappy's fans.

"I'd rather lose my right eye. He's not for sale," declared Mrs. de Shields, refusing all offers.

Napoleon was rewarded with an extra saucer of milk for each successful prediction. His public frequently telephoned for his advice—farmers wanting rain for crops, picnickers

not wanting it to spoil their holiday. Napoleon obliged with twenty-four-hour advance notice of any change. Disdaining the groundhog, coming out of his burrow annually to see or miss his shadow, Nappy worked full time all the year around. Never has a cat made the headlines so often. "Feline Forecaster Felicitated," praised the *Sun*, beaming on its favorite.

The weather-wise Napoleon never met his Waterloo. By 1936 he was hailed throughout the State of Maryland and beyond its borders. Nappy, folks maintained in a phrase of the day, was "the cats." He was close to his nineteenth year, a ripe old age, when death took him, and the *Sun* sadly headlined his obituary: "Napoleon, the Weather Cat, Has Forecast Last Storm."

"Nappy always liked blue," Mrs. de Shields told a reporter, "so when I saw the end was near, I brought my blue blankets and laid them around him. He died quietly and peacefully, without a meow."

He was buried in a pet cemetery beneath a stone inscribed: "Napoleon, the Weather Prophet, 1917-1936." Other cats succeeded him but none supplanted him in the family's affections and none possessed his powers of prediction.

RUFUS

THE TREASURY CAT

"A CAT MAY look at a king," runs the saying. But Rufus did better, for he gazed calculatingly at many golden sovereigns.

He was a large, sandy tomcat and a regularly employed civil servant of the British Empire. Proud traditions lay behind him; he was the sixtieth of his name to serve the Treasury.

With fellow cat employees he patrolled the rooms and corridors of the Treasury Building on Whitehall Street in London, and it was at the peril of their lives that mice ventured out of their holes to nibble at packages of banknotes. Rufus, an able and crafty mouser, lay in wait and pounced—and another would-be despoiler of His Majesty's currency bit the dust.

At first the sandy tom always brought his catch to the office of the head of his division, but when he and his trophies were picked up, carried out and put down beside the trash can in the hallway, the intelligent Rufus understood the proper procedure. Thereafter the charwoman found his prey of the previous night laid out in a neat row beside the can.

While Rufus may have indulged in a midnight snack and not have displayed all of his quarries but only enough to prove

BISH

himself the good and faithful toiler he was, it is true that cats should not be left to forage entirely for themselves. The best mousers are given regular meals, since otherwise hunger makes them too anxious to stalk successfully. That important fact was appreciated by the British Empire, which carried Rufus and its other cats on the payroll at a wage of fourpence a day each to cover board.

Now by 1930 living costs had risen, and as Rufus must have become aware, fourpence a day would no longer buy enough food to sustain a kitten, let alone a full-grown, hard-working cat. Perhaps it was with this discrepancy in mind that he, though ordinarily disinclined to sociability and having a mere bowing acquaintance with Treasury officials, decided to pay a visit to his Chief.

In Rufus's day and age you would no longer find the King in his counting-house counting out his money. Such was the task of the Chancellor of the Exchequer, and that gentleman, Philip Snowden, was seated at his desk, making up a budget which in American money would amount to $2,500,000,000—no less. He looked down to find a big sandy cat rubbing against his leg ingratiatingly. Having made his manners, Rufus sauntered over to peer at the coals flaming in the grate. He arched his back lazily, lay down, rolled over and presented his stomach to the warmth. Anyone could take note that a little more milk and cat-meat would warm that stomach internally as well.

Mr. Snowden recognized Rufus. He had heard of this cat which left daily testimonials by the ash can of his prowess as a loyal servant of the King. Consequently he shuffled through the papers before him until he found an item under State administration. Upon it he wrote, "Approve increase in cat's pay."

Everyone said it was due to Rufus that the budget provided for two pence more per day per cat, a handsome 50 percent raise.

The budget bill was submitted to Parliament, debated and voted, and in honor of his achievement Rufus was afterwards known as Treasury Bill.

CHESSIE

SLEEPING-CAR SALESCAT

Maybe a little girl had put the kitten to bed, as she would a doll, in her home in Vienna. Perhaps the gray tabby decided herself to take a cat-nap and leaped up on the cot. She crawled under the coverlet, laid her furry head on the pillow and softened into that complete relaxation only cats can achieve. One eye tight closed, the other narrowed to a drowsy slit, she "slept like a kitten."

Luckily an artist caught and sketched the charming pose before the kitten wakened and scampered away. For when G. Gruenwald had completed his portrait, and it was sold to an American gallery, the gray tabby was launched on a career which, though the artist would not live to see it, would make her one of the best-known cats in history.

She made her American debut illustrating an article on kindness to pets in the magazine section of the *New York Herald Tribune.* There she won the heart of the man who would name her Chessie and make her famous. L. C. Probert, vice-president of the Chesapeake and Ohio Railway, loved cats and kept a variety of them, along with dogs and other animals, on his farm.

He had been planning an advertisement telling travelers that they would sleep like a top in his road's new air-conditioned train, but Chessie changed his mind. One look at her and he saw that the proverbial top could not begin to compare with this small creature, slumbering so soundly and peacefully.

So the tabby that had dozed in a cot in Austria was put to bed in an American sleeping-car berth, and passengers were urged to "sleep like a kitten." Chessie was an instant success.

Letters poured in asking for her portrait to frame, and its exclusive rights were quickly bought by the C. & O. Models for pretty girls in the "ads" must have been moved to catty remarks when they found themselves outrivaled by the popular Chessie.

Her fan mail rose to movie-star proportions, and she was dubbed "America's Sleepheart." Besides advertisements, she became the feature of calendars, which were heavily in demand. Verses and children's books were written about her. Her likeness was a favorite pin-up in playrooms, battleships, and hospital wards.

Because of all the berths she sold, Chessie deserved a theme song—a lullaby, of course—beginning: I've been sleeping on the railroad all the livelong night. She also showed she could fill the job of freight agent, when one shipper promised five carloads if given a Chessie calendar as a bonus. Still more versatile, she acted as public relations expert and promoter of good will and performed so efficiently that the C. & O. was even given an extra name in her honor—the Chessie Route.

A new chapter in the story of her life unfolded in each year's calendar. Chessie's public, eagerly watching her career, sent delighted congratulations, when two kittens were tucked into the berth, sound asleep beside her. Since fathers ought to have some credit, Chessie's "old man," a proud tomcat named

Peake, now joined her, appearing appropriately on Father's Day. When Peake traveled, he yielded the berth to Chessie and the young ones and went to bed in the shoe hammock. In 1942 he saw his duty and with overseas cap perched jauntily on his head and steel helmet and field bag strapped to his back, he marched off to war. Chessie, asleep in her berth, dreamed of her hero being decorated by a two-star general.

Meanwhile Chessie was proving her own patriotism. Admirers, looking into her lower, found it empty except for a garrison cap and suitcase, but a grinning porter lifted sheets to reveal Chessie snugly asleep on a small pillow underneath the berth. She had gladly given her reservation to a soldier.

It was a grand day in the picture history of Chessie when Peake came back from war, bringing a captured Japanese battle flag, and rejoined his family in their regular berth. Chessie, after welcoming the veteran, went happily and traditionally to sleep, but nothing could prevent the two kittens from staying awake to gaze proudly and admiringly up at their gallant sire. Peake, striking an attitude, displayed for them the medal around his neck, his rows of ribbons, and a bandaged foreleg with an honorable wound.

For Christmas, 1947, the kittens got a toy streamliner train. While Chessie slept peacefully though the noise of their playing with it, Peake, not in the picture, evidently had behaved as more of a model father than ever. After showing his offspring how the train worked, he must have retired instead of running it himself all the rest of the day.

Chessie for years has averaged 50,000 fan letters annually. Four hundred and twenty-five thousand copies of her 1949 calendar were distributed. Her picture decorates writing paper for children and women's silk scarves. Friends shower her with Christmas cards, valentines, and gifts of catnip mice.

It may be that the tabby that posed in Vienna some seventeen years ago is still alive. If she has passed on and in cat's heaven is sleeping like a kitten, Chessie will keep her memory green.

FAITH

A CAT IN THE BLITZ

IT was a mystery why the scrawny, gray tabby with white breast and paws chose to settle down in the London Church of St. Augustine-with-St. Faith. Prospects for mousing must have been scant, since church mice are proverbially poor. Perhaps it was the peace and quiet, beloved by cats, and soft cushions to lie on, or maybe the tabby trusted that here the Lord would provide as He so often does for stray cats seeking a home.

The verger put her out, but the tabby had made up her mind and back she came, appealing to higher authority—the rector. Let her stay, the Rev. Mr. H. Ross ruled; she could live in his quarters on the top floor of the church house. Named Faith after the second patron saint of the parish, she fulfilled her religious duty by regularly attending services where she sat, quiet and attentive, in a pew or the choir stall. The congregation was proud of her, and she began to rival the reputation once made by the pet of another London church, St. Clement Danes, a cat fond of organ recitals, christenings and weddings, and considered good luck, black though he was, when he marched proudly down the aisle in front of a bridal couple.

Faith gave birth to a black-and-white kitten, marked so much like a panda that it was named for the Asian bear. It was 1940 and war time, with the bombs of the German blitz raining down on the city, but mother cat and kitten bravely endured the experience along with other Londoners until one day when the rector noticed a sudden fretfulness in Faith. Four times she carried Panda down three flights from the rector's rooms and installed her in a wall recess on the first floor, and as often Father Ross carried them both back until, after Faith's fifth move, he let them stay.

Had some strange instinct given the mother cat warning? Three nights later German planes made a heavy raid on London, and a bomb, scoring a direct hit on the rectory, plunged through the spot where the cat-basket had stood and gutted and fired the building. The rector, fortunately absent, hastened back and disregarded firemen's warnings to make his way to a vantage point where he could see into the blazing ruins. He shouted Faith's name, and at last heard faint mews answering.

There in the recess, miraculously still intact, crouched the tabby, her kitten shielded between her paws. "Her attitude and look," the clergyman declared, "said quite unmistakably, 'Why haven't you come to fetch us sooner?'" No panic for Faith. Though there seemed to be no escape through the fire ringing her, she would stand protectingly over her kitten till the last.

As flames began creeping closer and closer to the penned-in cats, Father Ross could hold back no longer. He seized an ax, hacked through barriers and, helped by firemen, crawled through the gap to bring out Faith and Panda, singed but unhurt. No sooner were they clear than the floor crashed through into the cellar. Safe in the church vestry, Faith licked her kitten lovingly, and her purring sounded to their rescuer

like "such a song of praise and thanksgiving as I had never heard before."

Though the brave people who saved hundreds of animals during the blitz asked no credit for themselves, they were prompt to insist that recognition be given the valor of dumb creatures, behaving gallantly under a terror they could not understand. So it happened that a special silver medal was struck by the People's Dispensary for Sick Animals, an organization with a record of fine service in war and peace, and the decoration presented with ceremony to Faith. Both the medal and a certificate, which hangs with the cat's picture in the Tower Chapel, bear these words:

"From the P.D.S.A. to Faith of St. Augustine's, Watling Street, E.C. For steadfast courage in the Battle of London, September 9, 1940."

BING

THE CAT THAT WENT TO COLLEGE

There was gay spirit and charm, even beyond the quota of most kittens, in the three-months-old brindle tabby, scampering about his cage in the Ellin Prince Speyer Memorial Hospital. He won the hearts of a boy and his mother looking for a pet to fill a void left by a cat that had strayed and never returned. They promised to give the kitten a good home, gathered him up and took him back with them to Forest Hills, New York.

The kitten and the boy, Paul Norton Williams, grew up together as fast friends, seldom separated. Often they were seen taking strolls through the neighborhood, with the tabby on a leash. Soon kitten mews developed into a voice that was so plainly a baritone with crooning overtones that the cat was named Bing in compliment to Bing Crosby.

Though Bing was not destined to star on the radio or in movies, it was not long before he found a place in the limelight. A big, handsome fellow with fine eyes and a glossy coat, he began winning prizes in cat shows. What if he was the offspring of alley cats unknown? Entered in classes for household pets, he carried off first honors, staring down pedigreed pussies

benched across the aisles. Every year when show time came around, he showed by his excitement that he remembered and was ready to meet all competition.

Once he disqualified himself by scratching his master, who, in his jealous opinion, was paying too much attention to another cat, but usually he brought home a blue ribbon, winning in his class at the New York World's Fair cat show and at a dozen others.

Such was his celebrity that on one occasion he was confronted by a rival, out to steal his reputation. Mrs. Williams and Paul, bringing their champion to a show, were startled to encounter a couple, exhibiting a brindle which closely resembled their pet and baldly announcing the pussy as the famous cat, Bing. Promptly the impostor was denounced and unmasked and he and his sponsors expelled.

Many cats have won prizes in shows, but Bing now achieved a unique niche in the feline hall of fame. He went to college.

When Paul was at Harvard, it was clear that his pet missed him around the house and would welcome a visit to Cambridge, so Bing, a veteran motorist, toured up with Mrs. Williams. First for a week-end stay, then for weeks at a time, and once for two months, Bing took up residence in his master's dormitory. Leash snapped to his harness, he and Paul promenaded through the Yard to the indignation of sparrows, unaccustomed to collegiate cats. Let Yale have its bulldog—Harvard now could boast a cat, which, though no official mascot, was a campus character. Bing enjoyed it all immensely, especially evenings in Kirkland House with Paul and his friends of the Class of '40. "It's always fair weather, when good fellows get together," and Bing, who had always preferred male company, was one of the boys.

He liked to attend football games, where he followed the play with that interest cats display in the strange doings of humans. When the backs crashed the Blue line, and Paul, a member of the Harvard band, cheered and clashed his cymbals, nobody doubted that Bing was rooting, too, for the Crimson.

Paul graduated and commenced a promising career, tragically cut short by his death from infantile paralysis in 1949. Bing, grieving for him, was never the same again. He had reached the ripe old age, for cats, of seventeen years and liked to doze long hours where it was warm, but he still took his strolls around the grounds, with a wary eye out for such dogs as the savage mastiff which once had nearly wrenched one of his legs from its socket. He never bothered about automobiles—their drivers usually looked out for him—so he was caught unawares by a laundry truck that backed out of the driveway and crushed him. Mrs. Williams picked him up tenderly and rushed him to a veterinary, but there was no hope for his recovery, and he was mercifully put to sleep.

It is part of many people's faith that animals share the hereafter with the human beings who loved them and were loved by them, and who would not like to believe that Bing and his master in the beyond are living over college days together?

SIMON

BRITISH NAVY HERO

Simon, a member of the crew of H.M.S. *Amethyst*, was a sober cat, true and attentive to his duty. He sailed not only the ocean blue but the clay-yellow Yangtze River. When big Chinese rats boarded in ports, Simon repelled them or fought bloody battles with them across the decks in the valiant tradition of British tars from the days of Drake onward.

The ship's cat was standing his watch below one day when the *Amethyst* received sailing orders. Conquering armies of Communist China, sweeping the Nationalists before them, had closed in on the capital, Nanking. The Admiralty directed that the trim little gunboat speed up the Yangtze at full steam ahead to relieve other British gunboats and carry provisions to the British Embassy. Simon leaped from his bunk, a petty officer's cap, and stood muster as a Royal Naval Animal Auxiliary should. His muzzle, chest, and forepaws gleamed white and neat against his black coat, and from the leather collar around his neck his identification disk hung shipshape.

But before the *Amethyst* could complete her dash upriver, the troops of the Chinese Reds had advanced to the north bank.

Their artillery caught the *Amethyst* in the bend below Nanking and opened a vicious bombardment on her and other British vessels, flaunting the rights of a neutral power and forcing all the small flotilla to retreat down the tortuous river, hazardous with shoals. All ships made their escape but the *Amethyst*. Battered by shell fire converging on her—her guns knocked out of action and her steering gear cut—she ran hard aground on Rose Island.

Simon took cover from screaming shells that riddled thin armor plate. Through the high-strung nerves a cat possesses he could sense the mounting tension, as the *Amethyst's* plight grew more desperate. Her captain fell, mortally wounded, and sixteen other friends of Simon's were killed and their bodies lowered overside to burial in the yellow waters. Lieutenant Commander Kerans, taking the bridge, put sixty of the crew ashore on the south bank to carry back a call for help to Shanghai and ordered rifles served out to fight off the Reds if they tried to board.

But, instead of Red enemies, four-footed boarders—big, ravenous rats—managed to swarm on to the decks of the gun boat from the island where she was stranded. Simon sprang to arms. With tooth and claw he pounced on them and scuppered them. The flash of exploding shells singed off his fur, and steel splinters wounded him four times in his face and legs. But Simon, never leaving his action station, fought one furious combat after another with the fierce rats.

Cruisers and planes, dispatched to the rescue of the grounded gunboat, were driven back by Red batteries. Great Britain, exhausted by mighty efforts in the Second World War and unready to enter another conflict which might bring Soviet

Russia to the aid of Communist China, was forced to leave brave men to their fate.

For three dreadful months the ordeal endured. Yet the *Amethyst's* weary survivors could still grin when they tallied Simon's score as at least one rat a day. His was splendid service indeed, since but for Simon's valiant battling, the ravages of the rats would have further depleted the ship's dangerously dwindling food stores.

At last the stranded *Amethyst* made repairs, and one night she slipped her cables and got clear. She fought her way through the Communist gantlet, breaking through a blockading boom. Safe at last at the river mouth, the crew spliced the main brace with grog by special wirelessed command of King George, and Simon drank his Sovereign's health in a saucer of milk. Lieutenant Commander Kerans, decorated for gallantry and promoted, mentioned Simon in dispatches to England, commending the cat for "his determined attitude which did much to improve crew morale and for behavior of the highest order during the whole of the Yangtze incident."

After the voyage back to England, the doughty ship's company of the *Amethyst* paraded through cheering crowds, but Simon could not be with them, since he was undergoing the six months' quarantine required of all animals entering the country. Yet Simon's day was coming. Reporters and photographers flocked to visit the hero, for from the hands of an admiral or the Lord Mayor of London, he was to receive the Dickin Medal, called the Animals' Victoria Cross. That decoration, founded by Maria Elizabeth Dickin to reward heroic deeds for King and Country by animals, had been conferred on fifty-three dogs and horses and one American-born pigeon. Simon would be the first cat to win it.

Alas, on the eve of the award Simon, worn down by hard service, caught cold and a day later he died. His medal must be given posthumously. They placed him in a little coffin, draped it with the Union Jack and buried him in a pet cemetery at Plymouth, his ship's home port, beneath a stone with a sculpture of his head in relief and the inscription: "In Honoured Memory of Simon, D.M." A Simon Memorial Fund was established for the benefit of his shipmates, disabled in the Yangtze battle, for the dependents of those killed, and to support the work of the People's Dispensary for Sick Animals of the Poor in seaport towns at home and abroad.

Today Simon's Dickin Medal hangs in the wardroom of H.M.S. Amethyst. Its ribbon's hues are green for the grass where dogs scout, brown for the mud and sand through which transport animals toil, and blue for the air, element of carrier pigeons, and for the sea Simon sailed. One bronze face of the medal is wreathed with laurel and bears the legend: "For Gallantry. We also Serve"; on the other stands Simon's name, his ship's, and the date of award.

No one can deny that Simon, D.M., was worthy and courageous kin to the Lion which with the Unicorn upholds the arms of Great Britain.

SCOOPY

CAT COLUMNIST

"ONCE UPON a time, I was a little tiger kitten. Like all good mother cats, my mother taught me to walk softly, to catch mice, and to wash behind my ears. I wanted to grow up to be a writer. Now my mother was wise. She said to me, 'Son, if you want to write, you can write in two places—an ivory tower or out in the world. And if you expect to live, you'll have to eat. But there are no mice in ivory towers, so you'd better get a newspaper job.'"

Thus—through a clever newspaperwoman who acted as one of his ghost-writers—Scoopy related how he began his career as cat columnist for *The Villager*, a New York City weekly serving the old communities of Greenwich Village and Washington Square.

"It just happened that *The Villager* needed a mouse-catcher," Scoopy continued, "and my mother knew it, so she said, 'The thing for you to do is take this mouse-catcher job and give it all you've got, and the next thing you know, you'll be running the place! And remember: don't be afraid to do more than you're hired for. It always pays off in the end!'"

That was first-rate advice, and Scoopy took it. He covered his mousing assignment energetically, and between times he did duty as a paper-weight, curled up in a letter box on the desk of Publisher Isabel Bryan. Though he seemed to be asleep, his nose for mice was as keen as any nose for news, and if a single one stirred, he was after it like a flash. No human with a broom nor any other cat could have beaten him to it. Like a newspaperman who gets a story ahead of rivals, the gray tabby scored a "scoop," and that was how the office stopped calling him "Kitty" or "Hey, you," and named him Scoopy.

Scoopy liked the bustle of the days when *The Villager* went to press. He appointed himself a receptionist to callers: artists and authors who loved the Village for the charm of its old houses and flats and its twisting, turning streets—householders who made flower gardens bloom in hidden courtyards. Mindful of his mother's advice. he helped the editor, the advertising department, and the man who cleaned up nights. So plainly did Scoopy prove that he was an important member of the staff that he achieved his ambition and was promoted from mouser to columnist.

He had always looked as if he would like to speak if he could and, like many a cat, he seemed fascinated with writing. It was Scoopy's good luck to have two talented newspaper-women write his copy for him—first Clara Bell Woolworth and later Emeline Page. They never signed their names but let the column. "Scoopy Mewses," run under his by-line and with his photograph. At the outset it sounded rather immature, as could be expected from a columnist little more than a kitten, but soon Scoopy began writing with authority. Naturally he covered the doings of neighborhood cats. "Pajah the Missionary Cat has gone to Oregon," Scoopy reported. "Junior Renay is back in Cornelia Street. His missus, Mary Renay, has been away on United Nations affairs, and Junior stayed in Detroit with his grand missus." "LST Mitchell is back in the Village, owning a garden in West Tenth Street. Seems there's a dog in the family now, 'young and fool but all right as far as dogs go,' and also a baby, but LST says he can't walk yet, so doesn't bother her. 'But I dread the day he takes his first step.' "

Still a columnist of Scoopy's scope could not confine himself to social notes and chit-chat. There were good causes to be urged, injustices to battle. Scoopy supported worthy community projects. He came out strongly for the American Society for the Prevention of Cruelty to Animals, and attacked the thoughtless inhumanity of people who go off on holidays and leave their pets home to shift for themselves. "It's a simpler thing than it sounds (taking 'em with you)," Scoopy advised, "and the reward is larger than the worry. Almost any dog would agree to a muzzle and almost any cat to a basket, if a short spell of these indignities guaranteed no separation for the length of the family vacation."

Scoopy's appeal for the United Nations Children's Fund was irresistible. Checks, bills, silver, and pennies to buy milk, sweaters, and cod liver oil for youngsters left destitute by the war poured into *The Villager* office. Five times over they filled the outsize China pig bank, dubbed by Scoopy the Honorable Martin Van B. Pennypig.

The fame of Scoopy spread until he became far more than a local character. His portrait was painted, and he was photographed opening a new telephone building. New York dailies, out-of-town newspapers, and national magazines quoted and praised the mews Scoopy mused. His fan mail was the heaviest in the office. Callers flocked in, and Scoopy welcomed

them with rather distant dignity but more cordially when he knew them better. Wrote one of his admirers: "He had the lofty detachment of a genius and the warm friendliness of a child. When he stared me down with a frigid hauteur, as he sometimes did, I could have been swept up in a teaspoon. But when he moved in on me grandly and condescended to occupy my lap, I felt as though I'd made the Social Register."

Scoopy was not far from his fourteenth birthday when his final column was written. "A day comes to each of us," it led off, "when we must leave our tasks, our joys, our responsibilities." Having done his stint, Scoopy, as newspapermen say wrote "30," that symbol which marks the closing of the last edition. "Death," *Time* sadly reported, "had taken Scoopy the Cat, the most celebrated literary feline since Don Marquis discovered Mehitabel." Sincere letters of sympathy from the many friends who would miss him poured into the office.

Today Scoopy II, another gray, striped tom cat, no kin to Scoopy but his spitting image, presides at *The Villager*. A typewriter beside him clicks out "Scoopy Mewses," and the column flows on. Wouldn't Scoopy I have wanted it so?